BROKEN
ARROW

JOHN WILSON

BROKEN ARROW

ORCA BOOK PUBLISHERS

Library and Archives Canada Cataloguing in Publication

Wilson, John (John Alexander), 1951-, author
Broken arrow / John Wilson.
(The seven sequels)

Issued in print and electronic formats.
ISBN 978-1-4598-0540-8 (pbk.).--ISBN 978-1-4598-0541-5 (pdf).--
ISBN 978-1-4598-0542-2 (epub)

I. Title.
PS8595.15834B76 2014   jc813'.54   C2014-901543-7
C2014-901544-5

First published in the United States, 2014
Library of Congress Control Number: 2014935383

Summary: Steve's romantic trip to Spain is interrupted when he undertakes a mission
to investigate what part his grandfather played in a bombing off the coast of Spain.

MIX
Paper from
responsible sources
FSC® C016245

*Orca Book Publishers is dedicated to preserving the environment and has
printed this book on Forest Stewardship Council® certified paper.*

Orca Book Publishers gratefully acknowledges the support for its publishing
programs provided by the following agencies: the Government of Canada
through the Canada Book Fund and the Canada Council for the Arts,
and the Province of British Columbia through the BC Arts Council
and the Book Publishing Tax Credit.

Design by Chantal Gabriell
Cover photography by Getty Images, iStock, Dreamstime and CG Textures
Author photo by Katherine Gordon

ORCA BOOK PUBLISHERS
PO Box 5626, Stn. B
Victoria, BC Canada
V8R 6S4

ORCA BOOK PUBLISHERS
PO Box 468
Custer, WA USA
98240-0468

www.orcabook.com
Printed and bound in Canada.

17 16 15 14 • 4 3 2 1

For Jen, my traveling companion.

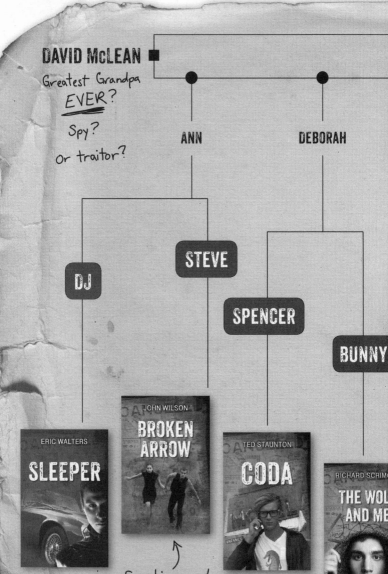

DAVID McLEAN ■

Greatest Grandpa
EVER?

Spy?

Or traitor?

ANN

DEBORAH

DJ

STEVE

SPENCER

BUNNY

ERIC WALTERS

SLEEPER

JOHN WILSON

BROKEN ARROW

TED STAUNTON

CODA

RICHARD SCRIMG

THE WOL AND ME

Driving a Jag
around London

Sunshine and
sabotage in
Spain!

Searching for
Bunny......

Skating
home

MELANIE COLE

VERA McLEAN

CHARLOTTE   VICTORIA   SUZANNE

ADAM

WEBB

RENNIE

SIGMUND BROUWER
TIN SOLDIER

SHANE PEACOCK
DOUBLE YOU

NORAH McCLINTOCK
FROM THE DEAD

On the road in
the Deep South

Channeling
James Bond

Nazi-hunting
in Detroit

**READ THE ORIGINAL
SEVEN (THE SERIES)**

www.seventheseries.com

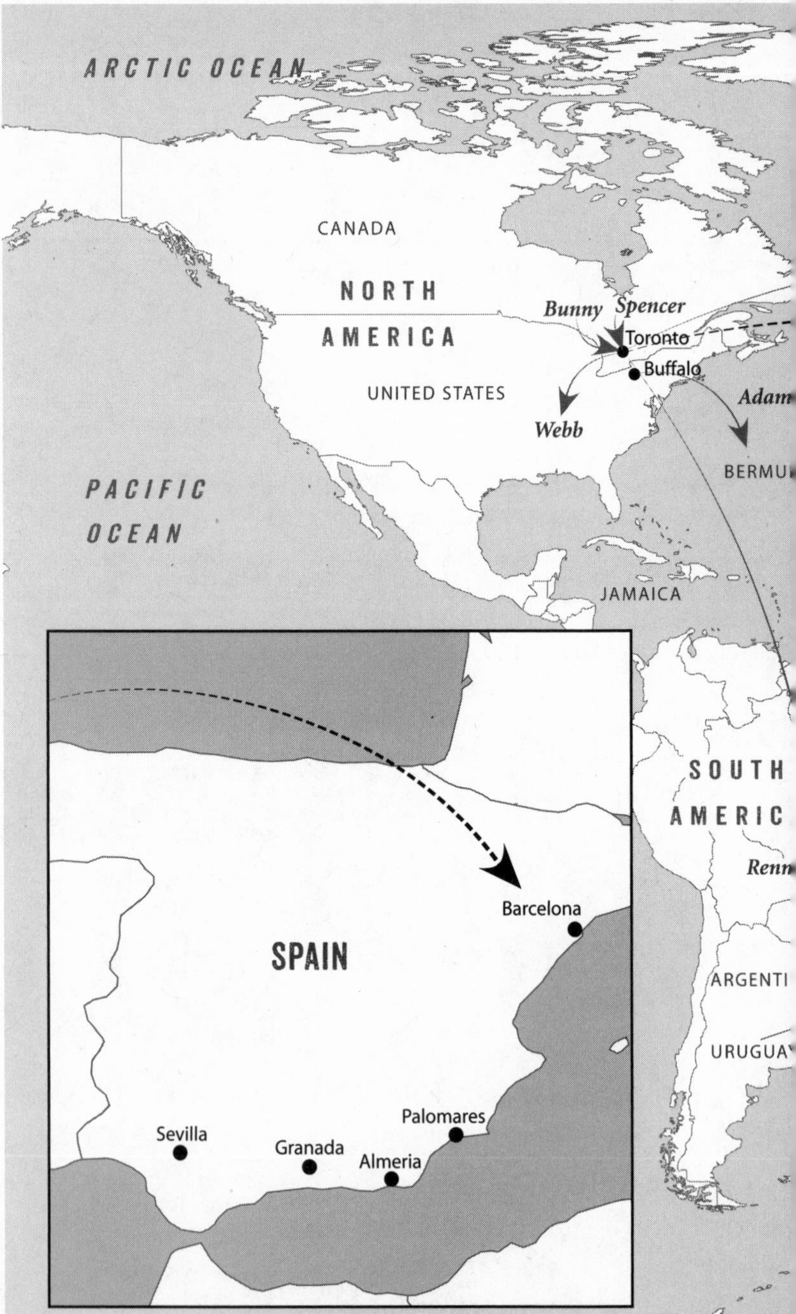
ARCTIC OCEAN
CANADA
NORTH
AMERICA
Bunny
Spencer
Toronto
Buffalo
UNITED STATES
Webb
Adam
BERMU
PACIFIC
OCEAN
JAMAICA
SOUTH
AMERIC
Renn
ARGENTI
URUGUA
Barcelona
SPAIN
Palomares
Sevilla
Granada
Almeria

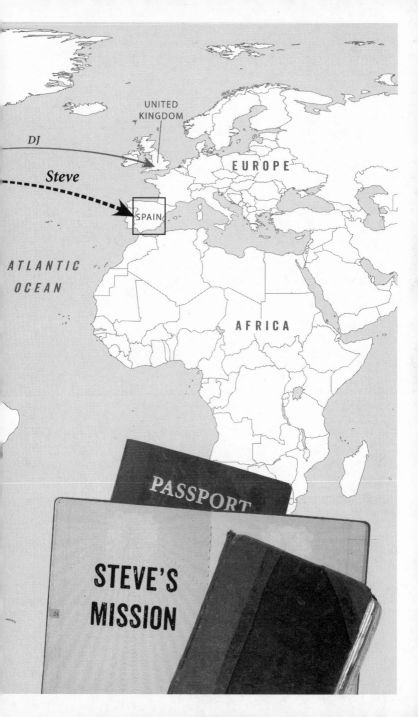

PROLOGUE

The man sat on a flat rock on a barren hillside in southern Spain, a pair of high-powered binoculars on his lap. It was much warmer than any January day in the man's home country, and the glaringly bright sun almost blinded him as he stared out over the blue Mediterranean Sea.

In the clear sky above, a white jet stream showed where a large plane was flying in wide, lazy circles. The man ignored it and kept his eyes fixed to the west. At last, he spotted something and raised the binoculars. Another plane leaped into focus. The man could see that it was a big four-engine jet with long, swept-back wings.

The line of white cloud it painted across the sky was heading straight toward him.

Lowering the binoculars, the man returned his gaze to the first plane. It had stopped circling and was flying in a gentle arc that would bring it onto the same course as the new arrival. As the man watched, the two jet streams slowly converged. He raised the binoculars once more. The two planes were very close now, the second behind and slightly below the first.

All at once the first plane lurched down toward the second plane. A blinding flash made the man cry out and tear the binoculars from his eyes. He blinked rapidly until the world came back into focus, and then he looked up. Where the planes had been there was only a fading orange fireball. Burning pieces of wreckage fell to earth, trailing long plumes of dark smoke.

The man put the binoculars to his eyes and scanned the sky. He recognized the tail of one plane, an engine and a large section of wing spiraling away from the explosion. Then he saw the orange-and-white parachute with a body hanging below it. Other parachutes blossomed across the sky.

The man placed the binoculars back on his lap. Everything seemed to be happening in eerily silent slow motion.

With the naked eye, he could only see the largest pieces of debris—the tail, the section of wing—but he knew there must be a lot more. Finally, a deep, booming sound reached him. He focused on the parachutes, not the few carrying men, but two larger ones. Each had a long silver container suspended below. One was coming down fast, the parachute only partly open. The other was higher and drifting out over the sea.

The man watched the drifting parachute, surprised that it was traveling so far while everything else was coming down more vertically. Then the debris began to land around him. Most of the pieces were small; the larger bits of plane and the parachutes were landing around the village on the plain below him, but one large piece crashed into the hillside nearby.

When things stopped falling from the sky, the man went in search of the large object. It didn't take him long to find it lying at the end of a ragged scar on the hillside. It was round and shiny and slightly larger than a soccer ball. Like a soccer ball, its surface was divided into interlocking hexagons. One side of the sphere was badly dented. The man stood for a long time staring down at the object, then stepped forward and attempted to lift it. It was extremely heavy, but by a combination

3

of dragging and rolling, the man worked his way back around the hillside to the rock from which he had watched the drama.

Many years before, part of the nearby hillside had slumped, forming a rocky scar that was so overgrown it was hard to see unless you knew what you were looking for. A couple of days before, an old shepherd had shown the man the scar and told him a local legend about the ghosts of long-dead Roman soldiers coming out of a hole in the hillside and stealing sheep. The shepherd had scoffed at the tale, calling it a "fairy tale to scare children," but he had found a hole that unwary sheep could fall into and blocked it with a large rock.

The man moved to the side of the scar and located a rock that looked less weathered than the others. With much effort, he worked the rock loose and shoved it to one side. A cool draft of air from the dark hole chilled the man's sweat-stained face. "Ghosts," he said under his breath and laughed. As soon as his heart rate slowed, the man mopped the cooling sweat off his forehead and set to work hauling the piece of debris up the slope and into the hole. A final push saw the round object disappear into the dark. The man listened as it rolled away. When there was only silence, he wrestled the rock back *into place. He scattered some dirt to make it look as if the rock had never moved, then sat down to recover his breath.*

When he felt better, the man went back to where he had found the object and kicked dirt and small rocks about to hide the mark where it had landed. He took a last look around and then hiked back over the hill to the next valley, where he had parked his small car on a disused dirt track. He glanced at his watch. The unexpected events of the morning had delayed him, and it was now midafternoon. He would have to hurry. He had a lot to do.

ONE

"With hedge-fund portfolio management, one has to keep up with evolving market strategies. It's not a simple matter of being aware of arbitrage mechanics and leveraging assets using derivatives—it's much more complex than that."

I think that's what the guy in the next seat said, although mostly it sounded like "blah, blah, blah, blah." I gazed out the plane window, wishing I could open it, crawl out and drop onto the snow-covered mountains below. At least that would be a quick end. Listening to this guy was death by boredom, one meaningless sentence at a time.

Since he couldn't use his cell phone on the short flight from London to Barcelona, he had assumed that I would be riveted by his explanations of how he made vast amounts of money by, as far as I could tell, doing no work.

My mind drifted back to the last time I'd looked down on the Pyrenees. That had been in the summer; now it was Christmas Eve—winter and the thick snow made the mountain peaks look like the stiff icing that Mom put on the Christmas cake. Thoughts of Mom made me feel guilty about not being with family at Christmas, but I got over it fast.

Mom had been upset back in October when I had told her I'd been invited to spend Christmas with Laia and her family in Spain, but two things had happened to distract her. A week after I had announced my plans, I came home from school one afternoon and found Mom and her new friend Rod in the backyard, each balancing on one leg and waving their arms about. Mom had met Rod in September at tai chi classes. I hadn't paid much attention at first; I was too busy thinking about Laia and worrying about getting through the first semester of grade twelve, but this was beginning to look serious.

"What are they doing?" I asked my twin brother, DJ, as we stood staring out the kitchen window.

"I think it's Carry Tiger and Return to Mountain."

"What?" I asked, looking at him.

DJ shrugged. "Or it might be Step Back and Repulse Monkey. I'm not too sure about all the posture names."

"No. I mean, what's he doing here?"

"Sorry," DJ said with a grin. "I thought you recognized tai chi."

"Were you born annoying, bro" I asked, "or did you have to practice?" My relationship with DJ had changed since our adventures last summer. His struggle up Kilimanjaro hadn't taught him humility, but it had given him a sense of life being more difficult than he had assumed it to be. "What do you think about the relationship between Mom and Rod?" I asked.

"I'm not sure," he said thoughtfully. "She seems happier than she's been since Grandpa died, but…" His voice trailed off.

"Yeah," I agreed as Mom and Rod, in perfect unison, turned, drew their right feet across the grass and swept their arms wide.

9

"Stork Spreads Wings," DJ said.

"But?" I pushed, ignoring the nugget of information about the tai chi move.

I stared out the window, thinking two things: how silly Mom and Rod looked, and how happy Mom looked.

"You know Mom and all the aunts are planning a Caribbean cruise over Christmas?" DJ said.

It took me a moment to realize he'd moved on from Rod and tai chi. "When did this happen?" I asked in shock.

"Couple of days ago."

"And I was going to find out about it when?"

DJ shrugged. "I've been busy. So has Mom."

"You could have texted me," I said. DJ was better after Kilimanjaro, but he was still the overcontrolling big brother, even though he was older by only fifteen minutes. "Looks like you're going to have a lonely Christmas with Mom and me both away."

"Some of the cousins are talking about getting together at the cottage over the Christmas holidays."

"Again, bro. When was I going to be informed?"

Once more, DJ shrugged. "You're not going to be here. We thought it would be good to get together and tell stories about Grandpa and our adventures in the summer."

"We?"

"Okay, it was my idea, but most of them seem keen on it. It even looks like Bunny might be out of juvie over Christmas. Too bad you can't be there, little brother."

There it was again, the annoying big brother/little brother thing. "You know I've got my flights booked already," I said. "Besides, let me think about this—ten days in sunny Spain with a beautiful girl versus a few days freezing and knee-deep in snow with you guys. It's a tough decision, bro."

"I just think Grandpa would have liked us all to get together. He was really into family."

"He was," I agreed, "but you've got to let go, DJ. Grandfather gave us different tasks in his will because he knew we were all different and that we needed to go our own ways—even if it didn't all work out the way he planned," I said, thinking of Bunny's experience, which had led to jail time. "But my path leads to Spain this Christmas. So have fun at the cottage and text me if anything exciting happens, like it stops snowing."

I'd probably been a bit harsh with DJ, but the family remark annoyed me. As it turned out, I wasn't the only cousin who wouldn't be at the cabin—Rennie was going to be on vacation in South America—but as Christmas approached, I felt a twinge of regret at missing the get-together. I got on well with my cousins, and we did have a lot in common. Besides, all the talk about the trip—how they were going to get up to the cottage in winter, what food to take, what they would do while they were there—made it real and made me feel left out. It sounded like it might actually be fun. Then I thought of Laia waiting for me at the Barcelona airport, and all my regrets vanished.

The time Laia and I had spent together discovering what Grandfather had done in 1938 had been special, but the two weeks after that had been amazing. We had traveled up and down the coast on our scooters, walking along beaches, swimming and hanging out in old villages away from the tourist crowds. We had even gone to Lloret de Mar to visit Elsie and Edna, the holidaymakers I had met on the plane out, and spent the evening in the disco in the Hotel Miramar. It had been a fun night, being entertained by a planeload of happy tourists from Wigan, but it was a relief the next day to head off along the rugged coast.

I had spent the last couple of days before my flight home back in Barcelona, where I had met Laia's mother and heard stories about her great-grandmother, Maria, and the time when she had known Grandfather. It was the best holiday I had ever had, and I was thrilled when Laia texted me and said her mother had suggested I come for Christmas. She proposed that I spend Christmas in Barcelona and then we could go down to Seville to visit her father. I thought about it for all of five or ten seconds before I was online looking for cheap flights. I still had the thousand dollars I had saved to travel to Europe this summer, a couple of hundred from a few weeks' work and almost another thousand from the money Grandfather had left me.

"Investment banking's very interesting." I glanced at the guy beside me, who was still talking. Apparently, nothing he said required a response from me. I guessed he was in his fifties or sixties, but it was hard to tell, and he certainly talked as if he were much younger. He could also probably afford the best in skin care.

Even jammed into a tourist seat on a cramped plane, he still looked like he'd stepped out of a magazine ad—not a crease in his suit or a hair out of place and a toothy smile that almost blinded me. His suit probably cost as much as I was paying for this flight. I wondered why, if he was so successful, he wasn't traveling in business class.

My mind began to wander. Maybe this guy wasn't into hedges or whatever. Maybe his perfect looks were a cover. Perhaps he worked for the CIA or MI6 or the Russian secret service, whatever it was called these days. What better fake identity than someone who was completely self-involved and unbearably boring? No one would suspect he was really a superspy—a James Bond out to save the world from international terrorists.

I smiled at my meandering thoughts. My companion misread it. "So you see what opportunities there are for someone like yourself to get in on the ground floor of this business. I could put some good deals your way. No pressure." He handed me a crisp embossed business card. "Name's Chad."

"Uh, thanks," I said, stuffing the card into my pants pocket. "I'll think about it."

"Just give me a call when you make up your mind. Cell phone's always on. Spending all your holiday in Barcelona?"

"At first. I'm meeting a friend there and then going down to Seville after Christmas," I said, feeling strangely uncomfortable giving this guy any information about myself. "How about you?" I added before he could ask another question. "You staying in Barcelona?"

"I travel all over," he said vaguely. "Barcelona, Madrid, Seville, Granada this trip. You know what business is like."

I didn't, but I nodded as the plane touched down. "What kind of business do you do over Christmas?" I asked.

"This and that. Import/export. I'll be doing a bit of real-estate work this trip. The markets never sleep. Seville's a great town. You been there before?" I shook my head. "You going to the beach as well?" I shrugged, although Laia and I *were* planning on a few days at the coast. "Plenty of nice beaches along the south coast. Good places to pick up girls." Chad winked broadly at me. He must have caught my expression because he hurriedly added, "Or maybe the friend you're meeting in Barcelona is your girl-friend?" I nodded again. "Well," Chad went on as we approached the terminal building, "the best of luck to you. And I mean it: give me a call."

"Sure," I said distractedly. I was looking out the window at the terminal building. Laia was waiting for me in there. This was going to be the best Christmas ever.

TWO

I ran from the plane all the way through the airport to the immigration lineup, not just to get away from Chad, but because I knew every step brought me closer to Laia.

The immigration officer scanned my passport, checked that I looked like my photograph, wished me *Bon Nadal* (which I knew from my attempts to learn Laia's language was Catalan for Merry Christmas) and waved me through. I smiled at Chad at the next counter—he seemed to be having some sort of difficulty with his passport. He gave me a smile and a thumbs-up. I hurried through to collect my bag.

My travel backpack was the last item to tumble onto the baggage carousel, and I paced in mounting frustration as cheerful, chattering holidaymakers, many wearing red Santa hats, grabbed their luggage and disappeared through the customs door. I had convinced myself that my bag had been put on the wrong plane and was halfway to Azerbaijan when it finally slid into sight. The only other piece of luggage going around was a very expensive silver hard-shell suitcase that I assumed must belong to Chad, who still hadn't shown up from immigration. Either he was trying to convince the official to invest in one of his schemes or he really was a spy. I strapped on my pack and rushed through customs and into the busy arrivals area.

The moment I stepped through the doors, Laia's arms enfolded me in the best hug of my life. I returned it and stood breathing in the scent of her hair, giddy with happiness. Mentally, I wished Mom, DJ and the others a Happy Christmas, but this was where I wanted to be. In fact, I would have gladly stood there all day, but I noticed Laia's mom standing to one side, watching us, a slight smile on her lips. Laia kissed me, and then we stepped apart.

"*Hola, la senyora Aguilar. Bon Nadal,*" I said to Laia's mom, summoning up the Catalan I'd been learning.

"*Hola,* Steve," she replied, her smile broadening as we shook hands. She switched effortlessly to English. "But please, no formalities. You must call me Sofia. It means wisdom, so I must be very smart." Before I could say anything, Sofia went on. "But let us not spend Christmas in the airport. Follow me." Sofia headed off through the crowded terminal and Laia and I trailed behind her, chattering happily.

"I am so glad you could come," Laia said as we walked hand in hand. "Was your mother very disappointed?"

"A little," I said, "but the cruise with her sisters is taking her mind off it, so I think she is okay."

"And DJ?" Laia gave me a mischievous smile. She knew all about my relationship with my brother.

"I think he'll be all right," I said, returning her smile. "The cousins, all except for me and Rennie, are going to Grandfather's cottage by the lake after Christmas."

"Are they going to have another adventure?"

"Not unless it keeps snowing and they get trapped for the winter," I said.

"Like the old explorers in your Canadian Arctic? Will they have to draw straws to see who becomes dinner for the rest?"

"Dinner?' I asked, slightly shocked by the image.

"I have been reading Canadian history," Laia said. "Did not Captain Franklin and others have to eat the bodies to survive?"

"I guess so," I said, "but my cousins will be fine. They certainly won't have to draw straws—DJ will probably decide who to eat." We both laughed. "I think Grandfather's will gave us all the adventure we can handle for a while," I added.

"I'm glad it did," Laia said, squeezing my hand. "I have a busy holiday planned for us. There is much to see in Andalusia—Seville, Cordoba, Granada— too much for a short visit, but my father knows the history, so he will tell us the best things to see. It will be a wonderful time."

"It will," I agreed. As far as I was concerned, as long as I was with Laia, whatever we did would be wonderful. Grinning like an idiot, I followed Laia's mom out of the airport to the taxi rank.

The Plaça Catalunya was very different from the last time I had seen it. In the gathering dark of evening, every building around the huge square was bedecked in multicolored, twinkling Christmas lights. In the center of the square, families skimmed around the ice of a vast open-air rink beneath a towering decorated tree, accompanied by a choir singing carols. Stalls selling food, ornaments and gifts were scattered round the edge.

"We thought you might like to walk through the square to get into the Christmas spirit," Sofia said as we got out of the taxi.

"And we have a special Catalan tradition to share," Laia added with a grin.

With the end of the school semester and all the preparations for my trip, Mom's cruise and DJ's excursion to the cottage, it hadn't felt much like Christmas at home. Now, strolling through the bustling, happy crowds, it did. We bought marzipan candy, nibbled on dried fruit, watched the skaters and listened to the choir. The one thing missing was Santa Claus.

"How do you get presents if there's no Santa Claus?" I asked.

"Santa Claus is for cold countries," Laia explained. "How would his sled land where there is no snow? We have the Three Wise Men, who arrive on January fifth bringing presents for the children."

"So, no presents on Christmas Day?" I asked, wondering when I should give them the presents I had in my backpack.

"Oh yes," Sofia said. "We have presents on Christmas Day. *Tió de Nadal* brings them."

"Who's *Tió de Nadal*?" I asked.

"You'll meet him soon," Laia said, and she and Sofia laughed. "But first, there is someone else you must meet." Laia headed over to a small stall at the entrance to a side street.

"We have different traditions here," Sofia said. "I hope you are hungry, because we have the Christmas meal tonight."

"Do you have turkey?" I asked.

"Of course, turkey and truffles. I have been preparing it for two days."

"Merry Christmas." Laia handed me a small box wrapped in tissue paper. Inside was a small porcelain figure. He was dressed in black pants, white shirt, red belt and a red-and-black hat. He appeared to be crouching down.

"He's very nice," I said, confused.

Both Laia and Sofia burst out laughing again. "Turn him around," Laia said.

I did and almost dropped him. The little man's pants were down, and he was…taking a dump.

"Say hello to Caganer," Laia said. "He represents equality—everyone from the greatest king to the lowest peasant must do what he does. He is always placed in the corner of a Nativity scene to remind us we are human. He will bring good luck for the coming year."

"Thank you," I said, wondering where I would put Caganer in my room when I got home and thinking I would have to get one for DJ. "I will treasure Caganer."

"Excellent," Sofia said. "Now that you have been introduced to our Catalan humor, let us go home and prepare for dinner."

Christmas Eve dinner was turkey, but not the golden roasted bird I was used to and had been expecting.

Sofia had spent two full days making a stuffing of the turkey meat, truffles, pork, veal, brandy and sherry and then sewing it into the turkey skin. The roll had then been cooked and pressed flat. We ate it in slices with apples, plums and fruit sauce. A host of rich side dishes and caramel custard followed. By eleven o'clock, it was all I could do to stay awake, so Laia and Sofia taught me Catalan songs until every church bell in the city tolled midnight. Then it was time to meet *Tió de Nadal*.

"Tió, meet Steve. Steve, meet Tió," Laia said, gesturing to a log lying on the floor in front of the fire. The log had a cheerful cartoonish face painted on one end and was covered by a large red blanket. "We have been feeding him candy for two weeks," Laia explained. "Now you must hit him." She handed me a stick.

"Hit him?" I said. "Why?"

"He has been well fed and must now be encouraged to give up the presents," Sofia said.

I tapped Tió on the back.

"That won't work," Laia said. "He must be *encouraged*."

I looked at the smiling log. The blanket stretched out behind the log and covered several oddly shaped lumps. I began to get the idea. "I will in a minute," I said and headed back to my room to get the presents I had brought for Laia and Sofia. "I think I need to get to know Tió a little before I encourage him," I said, crouching down between the log and Laia and Sofia and slipping their presents under the blanket.

I stood up. "There. We're friends." I hit the log hard, twice.

"Perfect," Sofia said, whipping the blanket off Tió. There was a pile of brightly wrapped packages behind the log. Like three excited children, we distributed the presents and began unwrapping them. I had bought Sofia some First Nations art from the west coast. Laia had been tougher to buy for. She had told me she would like something about Canadian history, but I had wanted to get her something more romantic. DJ had suggested a book about Canadian spies that he was reading, but I didn't think Laia was into spies. After a long search, I had settled on a book of photographs and quotes called *Canada: Our Century*, which gave an idea of Canada's history in the twentieth century, and a pair of silver First Nations earrings.

Sofia gave me a Barcelona Football Club shirt and a book of poems by some guy called Federico

García Lorca—fortunately, an English translation. Laia gave me a beautiful history of the Civil War, with hundreds of photographs from the time Grandfather had been in Spain.

I felt part of a second family and went to bed deliriously happy. Before I sank into a deep sleep, I managed to email Mom to say I had arrived safely and text DJ to wish him a Merry Christmas and tell him I hoped the snow wasn't too deep.

THREE

Christmas Day was quiet. We didn't go to church like many people, but we walked through the streets of the old town and down the Ramblas. I was happy to see that Laia was wearing the earrings I'd given her. The shops were closed, but many of the restaurants were open, and we stopped frequently for snacks. In the afternoon we went out to Gaudí's Parc Güell and strolled among the weird buildings and walkways decorated with brightly colored mosaics. The sun was shining, and it was very different from gray, snowy Canada.

"It will be warmer in Seville," Sofia commented, "and Felip will look after you well." I found the mention of Laia's father mildly uncomfortable, but Sofia continued without concern. "I think Felip is where Laia gets her interest in history. I prefer the present to the past. Perhaps that is why Felip and I were, how you say, incompatible."

"Felip works for the government," Laia said. "His department is in charge of helping all Spaniards become comfortable with our past."

"Reconciliation," I suggested.

"Yes, so that those on both sides of the war can feel a part of the same Spain."

"And not just the war," Sofia added. "Terrible things happened after the fighting was over. We are only just discovering that thousands of newborn babies were stolen from their mothers by the nuns and priests who ran Spain's hospitals under General Franco and given to childless Fascist couples. The mothers were poor or politically suspect and were often told that their babies had died. There were even funerals, but when the graves are dug up now, the coffins are filled with stones. All across Spain, children are trying to trace their real mothers, and mothers their lost children."

"That's horrible," I said.

Sofia shrugged. "It's Spain. After Franco died, everyone wanted to forget, but it's not possible to forget. We must remember everything, the good and the bad."

"And that's what Felip is doing?" I asked.

"Yes," Laia replied. "I am sure he will tell us more when we see him."

As we sat on a winding bench that was really a colorful decorated dragon, Sofia said, "My grandmother, Maria, never talked much about your grandfather, but I think she loved him."

"I think she did too," I replied, "and I think he loved her, but they were very young. He certainly never forgot her." I had let Sofia read Grandfather's diary before I'd flown back to Canada in the summer.

"What was he like?" Sofia asked.

"That's difficult to answer," I said. "I always knew him as an old man, and I still find it hard to think he's the same person as the boy who wrote the diary in the war. DJ and my mom both almost worshipped Grandfather, and I think I rebelled against that. No one could be that wonderful. Certainly he was extraordinary and did many amazing things, but he was more complex and certainly more secretive than we thought. There were things in his past, like his fighting in Spain, that he kept hidden from his family throughout his life. Perhaps there were other things that we still don't know about. Perhaps we'll never know."

I had surprised myself with this speech. I didn't want to leave them with the idea that Grandfather was a dark, mysterious, secretive person though. "One thing's for certain," I went on. "He treasured and loved his family above everything. That's why he gave us our tasks: to help us get started in life."

"I wish I could have met him," Laia and Sofia said at the same time.

"I wish I could have met Maria," I said. "What was she like?"

Sofia spoke first. "She was extraordinary. If one word could describe her, it would be passionate." Laia nodded her agreement. "I think she found it very frustrating having to keep silent while Spain was a dictatorship, but, living under a false identity, she had to keep a very low profile."

"A false identity?" I asked.

"Yes," Laia said. "At the end of the Second World War in 1945, Maria wanted to come back to Spain from France, where she had fled as a refugee when Barcelona fell to the Fascists at the end of the war. She wanted her baby, my grandmother, to grow up in this land, even if it was under military rule. She couldn't come back under her real name. The government was making lists of those who had helped the Republic during our war, and many were disappearing into labor camps."

"Or unmarked graves," Sofia interjected.

"Many, probably thousands, were shot," Laia agreed. "Maria had worked with the Resistance in France, helping crashed Allied fliers escape. It took quite a long time, but her contacts there gave her false documents. Until General Franco died in 1975, Maria had to lead a false life, swallowing her anger at what she saw going on and pretending to be okay with a government she hated."

"I think it was a tremendous relief to her when Spain became a democracy again," Sofia went on. "She could be herself at last, and she threw herself into all kinds of social causes, from helping single mothers like herself to protesting the presence of American military bases in Spain. She also struggled to get us to remember our past. She told me once that a country was nothing without a past—a complete past, with all the good and bad out in the open."

"So Felip is continuing her work?" I said.

"In a way, yes," Sofia replied. "Although he works within the system, it is very slow, and there are many political pressures that determine what he can and cannot do."

"But he tries," Laia interrupted. She sounded surprisingly abrupt, and I caught a look that Sofia gave her. Did they disagree about Felip's work? "He's working to get the Americans to pay for proper cleanup at Palomares."

"I know," Sofia said. "It's just that the process is so slow. Maria would have been out on the streets demonstrating."

Before Laia could say anything else, I asked, "What's Palomares?"

Sofia let Laia explain. "Early in 1966, an American B-52 bomber carrying four nuclear weapons exploded over the village of Palomares. Two of the bombs exploded and—"

"What?" I interrupted. "Two nuclear bombs exploded! Here?"

"They weren't nuclear explosions," Laia explained. "Just the conventional explosives in the bombs went off, but radioactive material was scattered over a wide area. The Americans collected all the bits they could find and dug up a lot of contaminated earth to ship back to the US, but most people don't think they did a very thorough job. Much of the soil around Palomares is still contaminated. Apart from the health hazards, the local farmers can't sell their crops. Even all these years later, the Americans still refuse to do a proper cleanup. That's one thing Felip's working on."

"Wow," I said. "I've never heard of that."

"It was big news at the time," Sofia added, "but now it's only a Spanish problem. That's why we need demonstrations, to make more people aware."

"You said there were four bombs on the B-52," I said. "If two exploded, what happened to the other two?"

"One landed in a stream and was found quickly," Laia said. "The fourth one landed in the sea. It took months to find it. When the Americans did bring it up, they made a big fuss, saying the problem was solved. And then, gradually, everyone forgot."

"I had no idea," I said. "I thought that sort of thing only happened in the movies."

Laia smiled. "Sometimes the real world is more exciting than movies. But let's not spend Christmas Day talking about bombs and radioactive contamination. There'll be plenty of time to ask Felip about all this in Seville."

"I agree," Sofia said, standing. "I know a nice little tapas bar where, so the story goes, Ernest Hemingway spent time during the war. I think we should go there, have something to eat and pay our respects."

Despite Laia's words, as we strolled out of Parc Güell I thought about nuclear bombs and accidents. I would certainly talk to Felip about it in a day or two.

FOUR

"Why did your parents split up?" It was late evening on December 26, and we had been on the AVE, Spain's superfast train, for five hours. We were only about half an hour out of Seville's Santa Justa station, and it had taken me this long to get around to asking a question I had wanted to know the answer to ever since I had seen Sofia give Laia that look in Parc Güell.

Laia thought for a long moment, gazing out the window at the olive groves speeding by. "They separated three years ago," she said. "What triggered it was Felip being transferred to Seville. Sofia didn't want to leave Barcelona and take me away from my school, but there was more to it than that." Laia used her parents' first names as comfortably as if they were close friends from school. It seemed odd. I couldn't imagine calling Mom anything other than Mom, but Laia had introduced me to a lot of habits I found strange.

"The whole process was very polite and civilized," Laia went on. "Of course, I was upset at the time, but there were no arguments that I ever heard and neither blamed the other. Felip has always been the rational intellectual, taking time to think things through before making a decision. Sofia is much more emotional and tends to react immediately. I think they simply grew apart over the years. They're still friends."

"Which are you?" I asked, "emotional or intellectual?"

"A bit of both," Laia said with a smile.

"But you miss Felip," I said.

"Yes, very much. We used to have wonderful long conversations about all kinds of things, from politics and religion to football and mystery novels. Now that he's in Seville, that doesn't happen so often. I miss our conversations."

"I love mystery novels," I said.

"There is no shortage of mysteries in Spain." Laia tilted her head and looked at me in that quizzical way she had. "I think you are very like Felip. You think about things and try to work them out."

I was pleased by the compliment. "I hope that's not the only reason you hang out with me."

Laia laughed and punched me playfully in the ribs. "Of course not." She leaned over and kissed me on the cheek. "I hang out with you because surrounding myself with dumb people makes me seem smarter."

"I'm looking forward to meeting Felip," I said, grinning like a fool.

My phone pinged with a text from DJ. I checked my watch: 9 PM. That would make it 3 PM in Ontario, so it was probably to tell me he'd arrived at Grandfather's cottage. It was, but it said something else as well.

Arrived at the cabin. Discovered stuff. Need to think. Will email tomorrow. DJ.

"Is DJ stuck in a snowdrift?" Laia asked.

"He's at the cabin," I said, my thumbs working the keypad of my phone. W@ u mean discovered stuff? W@ stuff?

"He says they've discovered something at the cottage," I explained as I sent my text.

"What?" Laia asked.

"That's what I've asked him. The only thing you might find at the cottage would be a nest of mice."

"Sounds delightful," Laia said. "Maybe it *is* just something like a mouse nest."

I shook my head. "DJ said he had to think about what he'd found and that he'll email me tomorrow. If DJ has to think about something, it's important."

My phone pinged again. `Money, fake passports, coded messages. I will send scans of Spanish stuff tomorrow. DJ`

I stared at my phone screen for a long time. What was going on? Was this a joke? I turned the phone so Laia could see the screen. She looked at me questioningly. I shrugged. "It must be some kind of joke DJ and the others have cooked up."

`LOL :-D Spencer's idea?` I replied.

A response came back almost immediately. `No joke. Weird stuff. Grandpa was a spy. We need to figure it out. More tomorrow.`

`Dnt lve me hanging, bro,` I texted. `A SPY?????`

"What does it mean?" Laia asked. "Was your grandfather really a spy?"

"I have no idea," I said. "We know better than anyone that Grandfather did things in his youth that he didn't tell anyone about." I felt my brow furrow as I concentrated, trying to remember anything that would help make sense of what little information I was being fed by DJ.

"After I got home from Spain last summer, I told Mom all about Grandfather's time in Spain. I also asked her a whole bunch of questions. I only knew him as an old man, but I also got to know him as a teenager through his war journal, and I wanted to fill in the bit between."

"Did your Mom think he might have been a spy?"

"No. This is the first anyone's mentioned that. Maybe DJ's got it wrong," I said, but I didn't believe it. DJ didn't get things wrong. "Mom said he was away a lot when she and her sisters were growing up. She didn't know what he did exactly, just that he was a businessman in some kind of import/export company." The phrase *import/export* rang a bell in my brain, but I couldn't place it, and I had too many

39

things to think about now to follow that train of thought. In any case, my phone was pinging.

Too much to send in text and I need to scan Spanish passport and codes. I will also send cash to your PayPal account. Letter says Grandpa was a traitor. It must be a lie. We need to clear his name. MTC. DJ

Both Laia and I stared at the screen, but could think of nothing to say before another text came through.

We've each chosen a place Grandpa was and the pages from his code book that seem to fit. Spain is one place and since you're there and like codes and mysteries, I'll send that to you. See what you can do. We've got a week to clear his name. Email tomorrow. DJ.

Laia and I stared at each other, and I blurted out, "I don't want anything to do with this."

Laia regarded me curiously for a moment. "Why not?"

I took a few seconds to organize my feelings into words. "Because I feel invaded. I'm on holiday, with you. I didn't ask to be involved in whatever DJ and the others have found. DJ's being overly dramatic.

A week to clear his name? What does that mean? It's DJ not wanting the wonderful image he has of Grandfather to be tarnished. I just want to meet your father and have a holiday with you, not go running off on some wild-goose chase." I was surprised by my reaction and by how strongly I felt, surprised that I really didn't want DJ intruding on my life this much.

Laia looked at me thoughtfully. "You are involved now, whether you want to be or not," she said. "Maybe DJ is overreacting, but false passports, codes, money and someone calling your grandfather a traitor? It doesn't sound as if DJ's making stuff up."

"Maybe not," I agreed reluctantly, "but I don't want this to overwhelm our holiday."

"It won't," Laia said with a smile, "and isn't there a tiny part of you that wants to know what it all means? After all, you *do* love mysteries. And didn't we have a wonderful time finding out what your grandfather did in the war?" I nodded. "Did that interfere with our time together?"

"No," I replied. "It gave us a chance to get to know each other. But it's different now."

"Yes, it's different now, and part of that differ-ence is that through the journal and what we did last summer, I have come to know your grandfather. Because of his love for my great-grandmother, he's part of my past as well. I don't want to think of him as a traitor, and if he came back to Spain, even as a spy with a false name, I want to know about it."

"I suppose so," I said. "And if I'm honest, there's a part of me that *is* intrigued by what DJ says."

"Okay," Laia said. "Let's see what DJ sends tomorrow. If he is exaggerating, we can ignore it. If the code is meaningless and we can't see anything that makes sense, then that's an end as well. But if it interests us, we can do some digging. It might be fun, and we'll be doing it together."

Laia squeezed my hand and gave me a smile that made me feel weak. "Okay," I agreed. The train slowed and pulled under the curving glass arches of Santa Justa station. I tried to push DJ's texts into the back of my mind. I would worry about all that tomorrow; now it was time to meet Laia's father.

FIVE

"We in Spain have created a culture of forgetting," Felip said. He was a short, intense man with black hair, olive skin and dark eyes that seemed to bore into me when he spoke. The intensity made everything he said sound important. "Half a million people filed past Franco's coffin when he lay in state in 1975. Now it is impossible to find anyone who admired or supported him."

"That's good, isn't it?" I asked. Felip's bright, open, modern apartment in the center of Seville was the opposite of Sofia's centuries-old place in Barcelona's Gothic Quarter. We sat at a polished aluminum table, breakfasting on croissants and drinking the best latte I'd ever tasted.

"It *is* good that people are not trying to bring the dictatorship back, but they are repressing their feelings. Not only that, but they are not allowing others to remember. Tens of thousands were systematically killed in Franco's repression after the war. Many, women and children included, were hauled from their beds in the middle of the night, driven out of their villages, shot and buried in ditches somewhere. Their families were never allowed to grieve. Now the victims' grandchildren want to give their ancestors a decent burial."

"Like Lorca," Laia said.

"Lorca?" I said.

"Federico García Lorca," Laia reminded me, "the poet who wrote the book Sofia gave you. He was Spain's most famous poet, but he was a socialist and a homosexual, so when the Fascists came to Granada, they took him out onto a hillside, murdered him and buried his body secretly."

"And his family wants him found?" I asked, feeling vaguely guilty that I hadn't read any of the poems yet.

"Oddly," Felip said, "his family doesn't want Lorca reburied; even they want to forget. It is the families of the other men who were shot with him who want to know what happened."

"It's complex," I said, struggling to understand all that I was being told.

Felip shrugged. "Spain is a very complex land with a very rich history. Sometimes I think we have too much history. But forgetting it isn't the answer. We must accept what we have done in the past before we can move on. Do you not have a similar situation in Canada with the Aboriginal people and the residential schools?"

"I suppose we do," I said. "I've never thought of it that way before."

Felip smiled. "See how easy it is to forget."

"Laia said that you were also working on getting compensation for the villagers where the four nuclear bombs fell," I said. I wanted to talk about Spain, not Canada.

"Palomares, yes. There are still a lot of questions about what happened there in 1966, but we're making progress. The Americans are close to agreeing to finish the cleaning they began at the time. In fact, I'm meeting an American investor there tomorrow to talk about the possibility of purchasing the contaminated land after it's cleaned up. Land is very valuable all along the coast, and hundreds of acres have been fenced off at Palomares for nearly fifty years."

"What's the contamination?" I asked. "Uranium?"

"Mostly plutonium," Felip said.

"Laia said that there was no nuclear explosion at Palomares," I said.

"That's right," Felip agreed. "We were lucky."

"Why didn't the bombs go off?"

"It's hard to be precise, because the design of the bombs is still classified information, but we think that the heart of the bomb was a plutonium core surrounded by uranium. It probably looked a bit like a soccer ball, a sphere made up of hexagonal sections. Each of those hexagons contained regular explosives. For the plutonium part of the bomb to explode, every single one of those explosive charges had to go off at exactly the same time. That would be unlikely, unless the bomb was armed by the plane's crew, and none of the Palomares bombs were."

"Okay," I said, frowning with concentration, "so at Palomares, only some of the regular explosives went off. Not enough to trigger a nuclear explosion, but enough to spread the plutonium around the area."

"Exactly," Felip said. "That's how the soil around Palomares became contaminated with plutonium."

"Plutonium's one of the most poisonous substances on earth," Laia said, her voice rising with anger, "and it lasts for thousands of years. The Americans *have* to do something to clean it up."

Felip smiled. "Laia, like her mother, can be quite dramatic. But she's right," he went on quickly before Laia could say anything. "As long as the plutonium remains in the soil, it's relatively safe. You can place a piece of plutonium on your skin without too much problem. The danger is if the plutonium becomes dust in the air and you breathe it in. Then it is extremely deadly. Only a few thousandths of a gram can kill you if it gets into your lungs."

"So plowing the land on a dry, windy day wouldn't be a good idea," I said.

"Probably not," Felip acknowledged. "I doubt if there are high concentrations of plutonium in the soil, but we don't know for sure. Much was kept secret in 1966, but stories keep cropping up. For example, there's a persistent rumor that there was a fifth bomb that was never found."

"There's still a plutonium bomb lying around somewhere?" I asked, horrified at the thought.

"Maybe not a complete bomb, but perhaps the plutonium core from one of the bombs that broke apart." Felip shrugs. "It's probably just a story. Secrecy is always a mistake. It breeds suspicions and provides a fertile ground for all kinds of wild conspiracy theories to grow. I don't think there ever was a fifth bomb. The Americans searched a huge area very thoroughly. I think they would have found something the size of a soccer ball, but the story got started somehow. There was too much secrecy back in 1966—and too many spies."

"Spies!" I exclaimed.

"Oh yes," Felip said. "A Soviet spy ship sat offshore watching everything that went on. There were probably spies on the mainland as well. Have you ever seen the James Bond movie *Thunderball*?"

"Is that the old one about the stolen nuclear bombs?"

"With Sean Connery, yes. It came out in 1965, and after the Palomares accident, everyone worried about the Soviets stealing the lost bomb before it could be found. It was all very exciting and dramatic, but then, Spain is a very popular place for spies. The English spy Kim Philby lived just two doors away from here during our civil war. He spent most of the war as a journalist on the Fascist side. His open sympathy for Franco allowed him to travel all over Spain, but he was really spying for the Soviets."

"Wait till I tell my cousin Spencer. He's really into spies and espionage," I said. "Didn't Philby go on spying for the Soviets after the war?" I asked, vaguely remembering a TV show I'd seen on famous spies.

"There were five of them," Felip said. "Philby, Guy Burgess, Donald Maclean, Anthony Blunt and an unknown man. They were called the Cambridge Five, although there were probably more. All were high up in the British Secret Intelligence Service, but were passing what they knew to the Russians. Burgess, Maclean and Philby fled to the Soviet Union and Blunt died in 1983."

"The number five seems to be the theme here," Laia said. "A lost fifth bomb, an unknown fifth man. Maybe your grandfather was the fifth man." She said the last bit with a laugh, but the thought had crossed my mind as well.

"Your grandfather was a spy?" Felip asked.

"No," I answered instinctively. "DJ and the others have found something at my grandfather's cabin that might have something to do with spying. He's going to send me what he's found in an email today."

Felip nodded. "Many strange things happened in secret during the Cold War, especially in Spain when Franco was the dictator."

"You said you're meeting an American tomorrow about buying land?" Laia asked.

"Yes, I'm going to drive down to Palomares to show him around. If an American businessman wants to invest in Palomares, it might help speed the cleanup process along. You two are welcome to come with me, or you can stay here while I'm gone and see some more of Seville."

I kind of liked the idea of us having the apartment to ourselves for a few days, but Laia said, "I'd like to come with you. Palomares is close to Cartagena, and maybe we could stop at Granada on the way back."

She looked at me with raised eyebrows. What could I say? "Sure. Sounds good. We can look for lost bombs and unknown spies."

Felip laughed. "I'm afraid it won't be that exciting, but we *can* go to Cartagena. It's just up the coast."

"There's lots to see there," Laia added happily. "Hannibal and his elephants set off from near there to cross the Alps and defeat the Romans at the Battle of Cannae. And Granada too? I'd love to show Steve the Alhambra. And we can visit the house where Lorca lived."

Laia grinned at me, her eyes sparkling with enthusiasm.

"Sounds awesome," I said, and I meant it. I'd gladly ride one of Hannibal's elephants over the Alps as long as I did it with Laia.

After breakfast, we went out to see some of Seville's sights—the cathedral, palaces, gardens. Felip even drove us across the river to the ruined Roman town of Italica, where the emperor Trajan was born. It was a great day, warm and sunny, but two things distracted me. The ancient history was wonderful, but, after talking to Felip, I kept wondering why there were no monuments to Spain's more recent history. I also couldn't stop imagining what DJ was going to email me that day. He could hardly have done a better job of piquing my interest.

I was disappointed when we returned, tired, to the apartment to find no email. We took a late siesta, showered and headed out to do the rounds of the tapas bars. Spaniards eat very late and nibble a lot. We moved around, ordering a bewildering variety of foods—Laia even convinced me to try snails with garlic—and meeting and talking to the people at nearby tables. It was a lot of fun. Felip could have written the Wikipedia entry on Spanish history, and he was interested in everything. Laia and I told him about our scooter tour following in Grandfather's footsteps. I had brought Grandfather's journal with me and promised to let him read it.

When Felip started asking about Canadian history, I began to feel as if I were sitting an exam and wished I'd paid more attention in history class. After a few stories about explorers, the War of 1812, Vimy Ridge and D-day, I was struggling, and Felip always wanted more detail.

When we eventually made it back to the apartment, around two in the morning, I was so exhausted and my brain so full of new information and experiences that I forgot to even look for DJ's email before I collapsed into bed.

SIX

As soon as I woke up on the 28th, I flipped open my laptop and saw DJ's email. There were five (that number again) PDF attachments. There was also a separate email from PayPal notifying me that two thousand Euros had been deposited and asking if I wanted it transferred to my bank account. That woke me up fast. If DJ was sending me that much money, how much had there been in the cabin? Where had Grandfather got it? Was it payment for being a spy, or money to carry out some secret operation?

My hand was shaking with excitement when I clicked open the email. DJ's covering note didn't tell me much that I didn't already know. He had no idea what the codes meant—mine or his—and he was sending me money. He did say he was flying to England and was going to stay with his friend Doris, but he didn't know what he would do there.

The first PDF I opened was a photo taken in Grandfather's cabin. It showed a hole in the wall beside the fireplace. Bunny was crouched beside it, grinning and pointing into the dark space.

The second PDF was a photograph that showed the table at the cabin covered with piles of money, passports, a hat, what looked like a fake beard and mustache, a small black notebook, a bag of golf balls and a pistol. Bunny was in this one as well, standing behind the table, grinning happily and holding a wad of money. It was all so bizarre, but it had to be true, even if it didn't make sense. Golf balls?

The third PDF was a scan of an old Spanish passport. It had been issued in 1965 to someone called Pedro Martinez and had been stamped for entry into Spain at Madrid airport on January 10, 1966. There was no exit stamp. I had no idea who Pedro Martinez was, but the photo was of Grandfather, older than in the photo I had of him from 1938 and younger than when I knew him.

The fourth PDF was a scan of an envelope, plus a handwritten page from a notebook. The words *You are a traitor* and *You deserve to die* were faintly legible on the envelope. On the page was written: *I hoped I'd never have to use this book, but I needed to keep my own record, my own account, in case things ever came tumbling down around me. Maybe I know better than anybody that you can never trust anything or anyone, and I needed proof of who I was and what I did. I just know that I always did what needed to be done. Nothing more, and nothing less.*

The fifth PDF had scans of a couple more pages from the same notebook. The pages showed a few letters and some intelligible words, but they were mostly groups of numbers. If this was Grandfather's record and proof, it meant nothing to me. In fact, since it was in code of some kind, it probably wasn't meant to mean anything to anyone other than him.

I sat and stared at the PDFs for a long time. I felt as confused as I had in the summer when the things Grandfather had left me tumbled out of the envelope after the will reading. At first they had meant nothing, but with DJ's and Laia's help, I had figured it all out. Could I figure out this mystery too?

I doubted it. That first envelope had contained clues from Grandfather that led me to a path to follow to get to the answer. Here, there was nothing to even suggest where to start. Grandfather had kept this record for himself. He'd probably never intended for anyone, least of all his grandsons, to find this stuff.

There was a knock on my door. "Come on, sleepy-head," Laia shouted. "Felip wants to get on the road early, so you'd better hurry if you want any breakfast."

"Okay, coming," I replied. I took the laptop with me and showed the email to Laia as I ate my croissant.

"Quite the mystery," she commented. "Do you have any idea what the numbers mean?"

"Some kind of code," I said. "See how most of them are written in groups of four? That's often how codes are written. That way, it gives no clue to the lengths of the underlying words."

"These numbers aren't written in groups of four." Laia pointed to several lines that were different from the others. I shrugged.

"Why don't you forward the email to me and I'll print out the attachments?" Felip suggested. "Then you can examine them to your heart's content in the car. But be quick. We have to leave soon if I'm to make my meeting with Chad."

"Okay," Laia said, finishing off her coffee in one gulp and standing up. "I've got some stuff to pack." At the door she stopped and turned around. "And bring the book of Lorca's poetry that Sofia gave you. If we get to Granada, it'd be cool to read some there."

"I'll bring it," I said. I'd sent the email to Felip and the printer in the corner was clacking away before I realized what he had said. "Who did you say you were meeting in Palomares?" I asked. How common a name was Chad in Spain?

"A guy called Chad Everet," Felip replied. "To be honest, he's a bit too smooth for my liking, but we'll see how useful he can be."

I had pulled out the business card the boring guy on the plane had given me.

Chad Everet

Investment Counselor and

International Real Estate Advisor

"I know him!" I exclaimed.

"You know Chad Everet?"

"Well, I don't really know him. He sat next to me on the flight to Barcelona. He talked nonstop about investments and hedge funds."

"That sounds like him," Felip said with a smile. "You'll be able to renew your friendship."

I groaned. Now I really wanted to stay in Seville with Laia, but it was too late. I collected the pages from the printer and went to throw my stuff in my backpack.

As we sped west across the dry Andalusian plain, Laia and I examined the printouts. The photos of the cabin and the passport didn't tell us much. We discussed the fourth PDF at length, but since we didn't know who had written that Grandfather was a traitor, and since the other message was so cryptic, we didn't make much progress. For many kilometers, we stared blankly at the mysterious pages from the notebook.

"The simplest number codes substitute numbers for letters of the alphabet," I said. "*A* is 1, *B* is 2, *C* is 3, and so on. So Laia would be 12-1-9-1."

"But that's not what this is," Laia said. "Your grandfather's code is written differently. There are no gaps to show the letters, so how would we know if 12 was *L* for Laia or *A-B* for about? Besides, each group of four letters begins with one, two, three or four. If those are letters, it's much too regular to be words."

"There must be a key. Some codes use a book as a key."

"Your grandfather's journal from the war?" Laia suggested.

"Maybe," I said, unsure. "It's in my backpack in the trunk. We can check it later, but I can't see how the letters could possibly relate to it."

We puzzled over the numbers for a few more kilometers but got nowhere. "What about the line at the top of the page?" Laia suggested. "It's not numbers."

"It looks more like a mathematics equation," I said.

FGL@=5pm

"Maybe five PM is a time," Laia said.

"How will that help us?" I guess the frustration in my voice came through, because Laia fell silent and gazed out at the countryside.

"Sorry," I said. "I hate having a problem I can't solve or a mystery I can't unravel."

"Not all mysteries *can* be unraveled," Laia pointed out, but she returned her attention to the pages. "So we've got the line at the top, which may or may not have a time in it. Below that we've got lines of numbers divided into blocks of four, each of which begins with one, two, three or four. Then we have ten lines of numbers not in blocks of four, followed by a large block with the numbers again in blocks of four beginning with one, two, three or four. My guess is that the first line is some kind of key to the groups of four numbers, and I have no idea what the other numbers mean."

"That sounds reasonable," I agreed, "but without the key, we're completely stuck."

"Maybe we should take a break," Laia suggested.

"Good idea." I took out the book of Lorca's poems and began thumbing through it.

"Read 'Lament for Ignacio Sánchez Mejías,'" Laia suggested. "It's Lorca's most famous poem. Mejías was a friend, a bullfighter who was gored to death in the ring."

"Okay." I was looking up the page for the poem when Felip suddenly swerved off the road into a rest area and braked hard. I was thrown against Laia.

"What's the matter?" she asked.

"Sorry," Felip said, but he was staring back at the highway. I looked out. There wasn't much traffic; a couple of large trucks and a few cars. As I watched, a black SUV with dark tinted windows sailed past in the slow lane. I couldn't see inside, but I had the odd impression that someone was watching us.

"We're being followed," Felip said.

SEVEN

"I've been followed before," Felip explained matter-of-factly. "A lot of people in Spain don't want the past dragged out into the open."

"The black SUV?" I asked.

"Yes," Felip said. "He was behind us in the traffic in Seville, and he's stayed there ever since. I've slowed down and speeded up, but he's always kept his distance. I pulled off to see what he would do."

"Who is it?" Laia asked, a trace of nervousness in her voice.

"Someone with a history they don't want uncovered," Felip said. "It happens quite often to those of us who are looking into the past—the lawyers, the investigators, even the forensic archaeologists we call in to identify the remains in old mass graves. We've all been followed at one time or another."

"What do they do?" Laia asked.

"Nothing much. There have been a couple of cases of investigators having their car tires slashed and one break-in that I know of, but those are rare. Mostly, it's just following."

"They're not very good at it," I said, thinking of all the spy films I had seen and the mysteries I had read.

"They're not trying to stay hidden," Felip said. "Quite the opposite. The point is to intimidate the investigators. To discourage us from digging too deep into something."

"What does this guy want to stop you doing?" I asked.

"That's what's confusing. This sort of thing usually happens when we're in the middle of a case and close to making a breakthrough. It's always been obvious which case the surveillance relates to. Right now I'm working on a number of cases, but either they're not controversial or we're in the very early stages.

"Of course," Felip added with a smile, "we mustn't overthink this. The people we're talking about are not noted for their intelligence. Are we ready to go on and brave the mysterious black SUV? I thought we'd stop for coffee and stretch our legs at Granada. It's about halfway."

Laia and I agreed, and we pulled out into the traffic. For a while, we both kept glancing nervously at the surrounding traffic, but finally we settled into our books. I looked up "Lament for Ignacio Sánchez Mejías" and began reading. About halfway through, I made our first breakthrough in cracking Grandfather's code.

I flipped back to the beginning of the poem and excitedly recited out loud:

At five in the afternoon.
It was exactly five in the afternoon.
A boy brought the white sheet
at five in the afternoon.
A basket of lime made ready
at five in the afternoon.
The rest was death and only death
at five in the afternoon.

"I see you have developed a taste for our poetry," Felip said over his shoulder.

"What happens at five in the afternoon?" I asked.

"That's the traditional time for the bullfight," Laia said. "The time Mejías was killed. That's why Lorca repeats it so often."

"Federico García Lorca," I read from the cover of the book. Laia looked oddly at me. "That line at the top of the page—*FGL@=5pm*—it means Federico García Lorca at exactly five in the afternoon."

Laia's mouth dropped open. "The key!" she exclaimed. "Your grandfather picked 'Lament for Ignacio Sánchez Mejías' as the key to his code. It makes sense. Anyone who knows about the war in Spain would know about Lorca, and the lament is his most famous poem."

"I guess so," I said.

Laia grabbed the printout of the pages of the notebook. "But how?" She ran her finger along below the top row of number groups.

1155 1761 4314 3123 3261 2214 3925 4331 2535 3141

"Every group begins with one, two, three or four," she said thoughtfully. "Let me see the poem." I passed over the book, and she thumbed rapidly through pages. "The poem's in four parts," she said, her voice rising. "What if the first number of the four tells us the part?"

"The second is the line," I contributed, being drawn along by Laia's excitement.

"The third is the word," she said, almost shouting now.

"And the fourth is the letter," I said. "Each group of four numbers represents a letter."

"Let's see," I went on. "One one five five. Part one. Line one—*At five in the afternoon*. Word five—*afternoon*. Letter five—*R*."

"One seven six one," Laia said. "Part one. Line seven—*The rest was death and only death*. Word six—*only*. Letter one—*O*." Laia rummaged in her bag for a pen and began writing letters down below the number groups.

The more letters she wrote, the more our enthusiasm waned. The letters didn't mean anything. We had the whole first line—*rotoflecha*. "It's gibberish," I said miserably. Then I had another idea. "Lorca wrote in Spanish, right? Grandfather probably used the original, not the English translation."

Laia stayed silent.

"We'll pick up a copy in Spanish and try again," I suggested.

"He used the English translation," Laia said eventually.

"But it doesn't mean anything," I said.

"He used the English translation, but he wrote in Spanish. *Roto flecha* means broken arrow."

I was excited and confused. "What does *broken arrow* mean?"

"I don't know, but at least it's words. Let's try the next line."

We worked together in silence for a few minutes. The second line also revealed some words, but they were equally obscure.

"*Cupola de cromo* means chrome dome," Laia explained, "but what a chrome dome is, and how it relates to a broken arrow, I have no idea."

"I do," Felip said, easing the car onto the access road leading to a gas station and a generic motorway restaurant. "This is as close as we come to Granada on this drive. Let's stretch our legs, have a snack and I'll explain."

"Chrome Dome was the name of a Cold War defense program in the 1950s and '60s," Felip said as we sat drinking coffee out of plastic cups in a burger joint that wouldn't have been out of place beside the 401 highway in Ontario. "Back in those days, the Americans were paranoid about the Soviet Union launching a surprise nuclear attack. The only way they could see to respond fast enough to deter such an attack was to have B-52 bombers in the air at the edge of Soviet air space at all times."

"All the time?" I asked.

"Twenty-four hours a day, 365 days a year," Felip said. "Every moment, there were dozens of bombers in the air ready to attack. They flew from bases in America but were refueled from bases around the world. As soon as a fresh wave arrived, the previous wave headed for home. Each one of those B-52s carried four M28 thermonuclear bombs, each one hundreds of times more powerful than the atom bomb dropped on Hiroshima in 1945."

"Like the ones that fell on Palomares?" Laia asked.

"Yes. And Broken Arrow was the code name for an accident involving nuclear weapons."

"So Grandfather's talking about the Palomares incident?" I said excitedly. "The Spanish passport would support that."

"If the passport and the notebook pages are related," Felip said, pouring cold water on our enthusiasm. "You don't know that, and there were a lot of Broken Arrows."

"A lot of accidents!" I exclaimed.

"Oh, dozens," Felip said with a calm I didn't feel. "Mostly in the United States, but in 1950, a nuclear bomb fell and exploded—not a nuclear explosion—over the St. Lawrence River in Canada. The worst two accidents that we know about were the Palomares incident and a similar accident near the Thule Air Base in Greenland in 1968, when a B-52 with four bombs on board crashed on the ice off the coast."

"I didn't know any of this," I said, suddenly feeling that the world was a much more dangerous place than I had thought. "What did Grandfather have to do with nuclear accidents, whether it was Palomares or not?"

"It *was* Palomares," Laia said. While Felip had been explaining Broken Arrows, she had been thumbing through Lorca's poem. "The next line of code is Palomares, and I think the line after isn't code at all: It's a date."

Laia showed us the page where she'd written *Palomares* under the code. The next line was simply two groups.

1701 1966

"The first group is the only one that has a zero in it, so it can't be part of the code we've worked out, but it could be the seventeenth of January, 1966, the date of the Palomares accident."

"You're right," I agreed. "Grandfather must have been involved in some way with Palomares, and he came to Spain as Pedro Martinez. The entry stamp on the passport says he arrived in Madrid on January 10, 1966, plenty of time to get to Palomares by the seventeenth. But why?"

"Perhaps the rest of the code will tell us," Laia said.

"Well, that will give you two something to do on the second half of the journey," Felip said, standing. "We should be heading off."

We gathered up our stuff and left. I walked across the parking lot, deep in thought. On the one hand, I was thrilled at the progress we had made decoding the numbers from the notebook, and wished I could boast to DJ about it, but on the other hand, what did it mean? We still didn't know why Grandfather had taken the dreadful risk of going back to Spain while Franco was still in power. If anyone had worked out his real identity and realized that he had fought for the International Brigades in the war, he would have disappeared forever into a Spanish jail. And did any of this have anything to do with the accusation that he was a traitor? Laia and I walked quickly, both eager yet nervous to see what the notebook said next.

We piled back into Felip's car and merged back onto the highway. I looked back at the parking lot and spotted three black suvs. I was becoming paranoid.

EIGHT

As we wound past the Sierra Nevada mountains, Laia and I worked on the notebook pages. It was slow going, decoding the message one letter at a time, and it took us a while to recognize that Grandfather had reverted to English, but we eventually ended up with a collection of seemingly unrelated phrases.

> *moron saboteur*
> *could not stop*
> *the fifth unknown*
> *hid so gorky would not find*
> *must stay hidden*

too dangerous
finding would be a larger betrayal
rock fall fourteen

"Does any of this mean anything to you?" Laia asked after we had stared at the phrases for a few kilometers.

"No," I replied. "It almost seems as if Grandfather is speaking in riddles. What makes the saboteur a moron? Are they stupid because they didn't do something Grandfather wanted?"

Laia shrugged. "Okay. Let's write down the question—"

"Or questions," I interjected.

"—or questions that we have for each phrase." She turned over the printout and wrote, *moron saboteur.* Beside it she wrote, *Who is the moron saboteur? Why a moron?*

"And what did he or she sabotage?" I added.

We went down the list and ended up with:

• *moron saboteur — Who is the moron saboteur? Why a moron? What sabotaged?*
• *could not stop — Stop what? Himself?*
• *the fifth unknown — Fifth what? What are the four knowns? Or four unknowns?*

- *hid so gorky wouldn't find* — Hide what? Who or what is gorky?
- *must stay hidden* — What must stay hidden? Why? From gorky?
- *too dangerous* — What is too dangerous? The thing that must stay hidden? Gorky?
- *finding would be a larger betrayal* — A larger betrayal than what? Betrayal of who or what?
- *rock fall fourteen* — A fall of fourteen rocks? Are there thirteen other rockfalls?

"That's a lot of questions," Laia commented when we had finished.

"At least we have a focus now," I said, trying to sound positive although I thought it was a depressingly long list.

"Several focuses," Laia said, "and we still don't know what the ten lines of numbers mean."

"Let's look at them again," I said.

372490

17798

372437

18120

372478

17911

371893

17021

373559

18601

"There does seem to be a pattern in the length of the numbers," Laia mused. "It's like one of those puzzles where you have to find the next number in a sequence. I can never do them."

I had an idea. "Maybe we shouldn't think of them as ten sequences of numbers. Maybe they're pairs: 372490/17798, 372437/18120 and so on. That would make five pairs and that might relate to the fifth unknown."

"Interesting," Laia said, "but we still don't know what they mean. 372490 and 17798—are they weights or numbers of…something?"

"Are those the numbers on the pages you showed me in the café?" Felip asked over his shoulder.

"Yes," Laia and I said at the same time.

"Read them out to me, slowly," Felip asked.

We had only managed the first four when Felip interrupted. "I know what those are."

"What?" we shouted from the backseat.

Felip picked his handheld GPS off the dash and tossed it back to us. "Plug them into this," he said. "Your numbers are locations—latitude and longitude—37 degrees 24 minutes 90 seconds north and 1 degree 77 minutes 98 seconds west."

"Five locations," Laia shouted triumphantly. She hunched over the GPS and punched numbers in while I peered at the screen, holding my breath. The machine sat for what seemed an age and then a map appeared with a tiny red cross on it—right beside the village of Palomares.

"It's in Palomares," Laia said breathlessly.

The next two locations formed a line right through Palomares. "There must be a mistake," Laia said when the fourth location showed nothing but a red cross on a blue background. "There's nothing here."

"Can you change the scale on this?" I asked. Laia pressed some buttons and a coastline appeared. The red cross was about eight kilometers offshore. "Those must be the locations of the four bombs from the B-52. Three landed around Palomares and the fourth fell in the sea and took months to find. Where's the last location?"

Once more Laia's fingers worked. The final red cross was in the hills, a few kilometers inland from Palomares. "The four known and the fifth unknown?" I speculated.

"I'm sure it's the four known bombs," Laia said, "but there wasn't a fifth one. Felip, could there have been a fifth bomb on board the B-52?"

He shook his head. "No. Throughout Chrome Dome, every B-52 carried four bombs, each of which had a specified target inside the Soviet Union if they were ordered to fly in."

"What if it's not a complete bomb but the plutonium core from one of the four that broke apart?" I asked.

"It's possible," Felip said, but he sounded far from convinced. "The Americans found three bombs in the first twenty-four hours. It would have been obvious if something as large as the plutonium core was missing, and they would have found it. It was the size of a soccer ball, and they searched everywhere— photographs from the time show lines of men in masks, shoulder to shoulder, walking over the land- scape. They would have found it."

"Unless it was hidden," Laia said. "Hidden so that 'gorky' couldn't find it."

"Now you've been reading too many mystery stories," Felip said with a laugh. "There weren't spies running all over the hills like in one of your James Bond movies."

"You said there was a Soviet spy ship and probably spies on land," I pointed out. Felip nodded slowly. "And why did the Americans spend such a long time searching around Palomares if they found the first three bombs on the first day and the fourth was underwater?" I asked.

"They wanted to clean up everything," Felip said, but he didn't sound quite so certain. "There were many pieces of the two planes that had to be cleaned up as well."

"But they *could* have been looking for a fifth bomb," I said.

"It's possible, I suppose. But why then did they leave without it?"

"Maybe they took it with them and didn't tell anyone," I said. "Maybe they thought someone else had found it, or maybe they just didn't want more of a fuss. They didn't want to look even more stupid after it took them so long to find and bring up the fourth bomb. Perhaps they thought if they couldn't find it, no one could."

"It's all a bit of a stretch," Felip said.

"Okay," Laia joined in, "but can we go and look while we're in Palomares? It won't take long with the GPS."

Felip sighed. I suspected this wasn't the first time Laia had talked him into doing something unplanned. "If there's time," he said.

Laia turned to look at me, smiled and winked broadly.

"I saw that," Felip said. I glanced at the rear-view mirror. I could tell from Felip's eyes that he was smiling too.

"So," Laia said, "the fifth unknown is part of a bomb…"

"Possibly," Felip said from the front.

Laia grimaced, but she continued, "Possibly, the fifth unknown is part of a bomb. The four knowns are the four known bombs at Palomares." She waited and looked pointedly at the back of Felip's head. He said nothing, fixing his eyes on the road ahead.

"The fifth bomb landed in the hills and was hidden from gorky because it was too dangerous."

"And the bomb was hidden behind the fourteenth rockfall," I said, worried that we were building too much of our story on speculation. "We're guessing at an awful lot. And how does the stupid saboteur fit into this?"

Felip laughed. "You think the saboteur was stupid?"

"Yes," I said indignantly. "That's what *moron* means."

"I know," Felip agreed, laughter still in his voice, "but *Base Aérea de Morón* is an American Air Force base outside Seville." Laia and I stared at her father. "What is more," Felip went on, "Morón is where the refueling planes left from to meet up with the returning B-52s in 1966."

"So there was a saboteur—who's not stupid— at Morón Air Base, planning to bring down a B-52 over Spain in 1966." Laia was speaking quickly as she continued to build our theory. "He or she succeeds, and four or five bombs fall over Palomares."

Laia looked at me with a triumphant smile on her face. I couldn't share her excitement. What if Grandfather was the saboteur? What if he really was a traitor?

NINE

"Palomares has changed a lot since 1966," Felip explained as we stood beside a high wire fence with several *Beware Radiation* signs on it. "Back then it was a dusty village of a few hundred people who made a living growing tomatoes. Now…" Felip's voice trailed off, but it was obvious what he meant as he waved his hand toward the glistening Mediterranean. The blue water two kilometers away was just visible between white-painted villas and resort hotels lining the beach.

"It's the Spanish miracle," Felip continued, his voice heavy with irony. "In forty years, we have created one of the largest cities in Europe—in a long, thin strip from Gibraltar to France—and most of the residents are not Spanish. Tens of thousands of aged northern Europeans who want to retire in the sun live here year-round, and millions who want to escape for a couple of weeks in the summer visit. It's probably easier to get fish and chips and English beer here than in Canada."

"And Chad Everet wants to build a new resort here?" I pointed through the fence at the unprom-ising-looking scrub.

"He is a man of vision," Felip said, "and he's punctual." I looked to where he was pointing and saw a cloud of dust rising from the dirt track we had followed from the main road.

"This isn't one of the locations," Laia said. She had been busy with Felip's GPS ever since we'd arrived. Her brow was furrowed in concentration. "Are we wrong about the numbers being the bomb locations?"

"No," Felip said. "None of the bombs fell here. The wind blew some plutonium contamination here from the explosion of number two. Look, I'm going to be tied up with this guy for a couple of hours. If you walk back into town, you pass the places where bombs number one and three fell. The GPS will tell you where. You can't miss it: the road is Calle las Bombardas—the street of the bombers. There's a café on the edge of town called Pedro's. I'll meet you there in about two hours."

"Sounds good," Laia said.

A sleek silver BMW Z4 pulled up beside Felip's vehicle. The door opened and Chad stepped out and stretched. "*Buenas tardes, señor Aguilar. ¿Cómo estás?*" he said in a polished Spanish accent as he held out his hand.

Felip shook Chad's hand and replied in equally flawless English. "I'm well, thank you. I trust you had no trouble finding us."

"None at all. Always rely on the good old GPS." Chad's gaze flicked over Laia and rested on me. "And I believe I know you," he said.

"We met on the plane," I said as we shook hands. His hand was smooth and dry, even in the afternoon heat. It made my hand feel grubby and clammy.

"I remember. Good to meet you again, Steve. And this must be your friend from Barcelona." He shook hands with Laia.

"My daughter, Laia," Felip said. "They're just heading into town to do some looking around while we get on with business."

"Perfect," Chad said, flashing his expensive teeth. "You kids have fun."

"Thanks," I said as Laia and I turned and headed toward the road.

"What a smooth operator," Laia said as soon as we were out of earshot.

"He's the most boring person I've ever met," I said. "And there's something about him I don't trust."

"Yeah, he's *too* smooth," Laia agreed. "Still, if he helps the people of Palomares get all the radioactivity cleaned up, that's good."

I nodded. "The area looks pretty depressed." The low, dry hills around us were crisscrossed by truck and ATV trails. Strange pieces of rusted machinery dotted the landscape, and farther off I could see broken-down walls and chimneys from what I assumed were abandoned factories. It looked like a film set from an end-of-the-world movie.

"More than two thousand years ago, this was one of the richest places in the world. There are hundreds of old mines in the hills around here, and the silver from them made Carthage the most powerful nation in the Mediterranean—until the Romans defeated them and took over the mines, and then they became the most powerful nation."

"Has there been mining more recently?" I asked, looking at the ruins in the distance.

"Some," Laia said, "but nothing like in ancient times."

We walked along the dirt road in silence for a while, just happy to be together. Then something that had been nagging at the back of my mind crystallized. I stopped. "Chad knew my name."

"You met him before," Laia pointed out. "You must have told him on the plane."

"I didn't," I said. "I barely said anything to him on the plane. He did all the talking. Even then, I didn't trust him."

"Maybe Felip told him," Laia said as we began walking again. "He must have said we'd be here with him for the meeting."

"I guess," I said, "although I can't see why Felip would mention my name. And anyway, don't you think it's quite the coincidence that the person who sat beside me on the plane should turn up here for a business meeting with Felip?"

"Coincidences happen. What are you suggesting—that there's a huge conspiracy around your visit here? That's even wilder than our interpretation of your grandfather's code. There's no conspiracy, and whatever happened all those years ago is forgotten. It's interesting to try and work it all out, but that's all."

"I suppose you're right," I said. What Laia said made sense, but there had to be something else going on. The coincidences were piling up, and the only common link I could see was Grandfather's coded message.

"This is where the first bomb fell." We had reached a narrow paved road, and Laia was standing looking at a shallow streambed. "It's the one that landed intact because its parachute opened in time to slow its fall. So if bomb number five *is* the plutonium core from one of the four known bombs, then it's not from this one. The tail section of the B-52 landed up there." Laia pointed up the small valley. There was nothing to show that anything unusual—especially one of the most serious nuclear accidents ever—had disturbed this unremarkable spot. Only the flickering numbers on the GPS and what we had learned from Felip and a couple of quick Internet searches told us where we were and what had happened here.

"What must it have been like that day?" I wondered out loud as we walked on. "An explosion in the sky, then flaming wreckage, bodies and four nuclear bombs raining from the heavens on this sleepy village. I read on one of the websites that one of the first Americans to arrive found the villagers picking up pieces of the dead crew members and trying to work out which part went with which body."

We walked in silence, imagining the horror of that January morning. The focus of what we'd read had always been on the four nuclear bombs and the search for them. The human element had often been missed. Seven men—the entire four-man crew of the refueling plane from Morón Air Base and three of the B-52 crew—had died, their bodies horribly mutilated, either in the fiery explosion or the fall from 30,000 feet. Large pieces of flaming wreckage had landed all around the village—miraculously, missing the local school and any houses. In seconds, the lives of everyone in an entire community had changed forever.

It was a horrifying tragedy, but I couldn't get my personal worries out of my mind. DJ and the others had certainly discovered something about Grandfather that he had managed to keep secret from his close family. Had it been something sinister? I wondered what the cousins were doing and what they had discovered. I made a mental note to text DJ that evening to let him know what we had found out so far. I wished I could talk to him. He was always so rational and sure. Even when he was wrong, he sounded right, and that was comforting. But he wasn't here. He was chasing his own mysteries in England.

"Do you think Grandfather might have been the saboteur at Morón?" I blurted out.

Laia stopped and stared at me. "You don't honestly believe that could be possible, do you?" she asked.

"I don't know." I shrugged. "I'm really confused. Grandfather certainly had a whole secret life, and someone thought he was a traitor."

"Steve, sometimes you think too much," Laia said. "Can you see the young man who fought against the Fascists being a traitor?" I shook my head. "Or the old man who put so much thought into giving each of his grandsons the perfect task?" Again I shook my head. "Then those are the things you have to hold in your mind. The grandfather you knew couldn't be a traitor, so whoever wrote that must be wrong."

"I guess so," I said. I loved Laia for being so certain, but it wasn't that simple. "What do we really know about what the world was like back in 1966? People thought the world was on the brink of destruction and that all they had to look forward to, if they were lucky, was surviving in a nuclear waste-land. Revolution was in the air. What if Grandfather tried to sabotage something at the air base to bring attention to the dangers of the Chrome Dome project and it went horribly wrong?"

"I can't believe that," Laia said, her eyes boring into me until I felt distinctly uncomfortable. "Your grandfather would never have done anything that put people's lives in danger, even for what he thought was a good cause."

I stopped myself from pointing out that in his journal from 1938, he had talked about possibly shooting an enemy soldier. That had been in a war though. That was different, wasn't it?

We walked on and found the site where bomb number three had fallen. Again, there was nothing to see at the GPS location—but then, this bomb had exploded, so there hadn't been much to see even in 1966. "If what we're calling bomb number five—the plutonium trigger bomb—had been part of this bomb, or of bomb number two," I said, "and they both exploded when they hit the ground, how could there have been a trigger bomb thrown into the hills?"

Laia looked at the dry ground thoughtfully. "Okay," she said. "Everyone assumes that bombs two and three exploded when they landed. That makes sense with bomb number two, because it spread a lot of plutonium over a very large area, but with bomb number three, there was very little contamination."

"Perhaps the explosion wasn't as bad."

"Perhaps. Or perhaps bomb number three broke apart in the air. If that happened, then the plutonium core could have gone anywhere."

I looked up into the peaceful blue sky, trying to imagine bits of the most powerful bombs the world had ever seen flying all over the place. "Maybe we'll find out when we go to location five tomorrow."

"I hope so," Laia said, "but right now, we're at the edge of town. Pedro's can't be far, and I could use a cold drink." She glanced at her watch. "Felip won't be here for over an hour; maybe we could go and look for bomb two after our drink."

"Great idea," I said. We set off, talking happily about nothing in particular, both of us relieved to spend a few minutes not discussing death and destruction. We were in among the neat whitewashed houses when a black SUV with tinted windows appeared around the corner ahead of us.

TEN

I think we would have stopped and stared even if we hadn't recognized the vehicle. Its bulk almost filled the narrow road, a black, threatening shape amidst the bright white buildings.

"Is that the car that was following us?" Laia asked, although we both knew the answer.

"Let's go back," I said. I had a vague idea of ducking into a doorway or between a couple of buildings, but we never got the chance. I turned and crashed into a mountain of a man. It was like hitting a brick wall. He was over six feet tall and almost as broad across the shoulders. His head was shaved, and he wore dark glasses and a loose black suit. A scar ran across his cheek from his nose to just below his ear. He was a threatening figure, but it was what I felt under his jacket that made me certain I would obey whatever command he gave me. I had felt it for only a second, but I was convinced he was wearing a gun in a shoulder holster.

"Let us past," Laia ordered. She tried to push past him, but he put a massive hand on her shoulder and, without apparent effort, held her in place. She kicked him in the shin, and he didn't flinch.

I was considering trying to kick him somewhere that would hurt more when the SUV pulled up alongside us. The back door opened. "In," Scarface said. Not seeing much of an alternative, we obeyed. He climbed in beside us, squashing us against the far door, and we moved off.

The guy driving could have been Scarface's twin brother—shaved head, dark glasses, black suit—except that his head was covered with complex, swirling tattoos. There was a much smaller figure sitting in the passenger seat.

"This is kidnapping," Laia said. "You could get life in prison." I admired Laia's spirit but doubted she was telling these guys anything they didn't already know.

The guy in the passenger seat turned to look at us. His skin was so weather-beaten it was tough to tell his age, but he was older than the other two. His gray hair and beard were cropped very short, and his eyes were a strange pale, watery blue. "I don't like to think of it as kidnapping," he said with a friendly smile. "Let us just say that I desire a companionable—how do you say in English?—chat, and I think that might be best achieved in peace and quiet, away from prying eyes." He had a soft voice that, combined with a heavy accent—Russian, I thought—made it necessary to concentrate on what he was saying.

"Stop the vehicle and let us out right now," Laia ordered.

The old man laughed softly. "My dear Laia," he said, "I fear that is not possible at this time."

"How do you know her name?" I asked.

"I know many things, Steve, but I think this is enough conversation for now. We will have a chance to talk in peace and quiet when we get where we are going."

"Where are we going? What do you want with us?" Laia asked.

"Silence!" Scarface ordered. We obeyed and sat quietly, holding hands tightly while Tattoo Head drove us into the hills.

Oddly, as we drove out of Palomares, I didn't feel afraid. For all I knew, these men were going to murder us and bury us in shallow graves that would never be found. But that made no sense—I could see no reason why they would want to kill us. Besides, the older guy—I thought of him as Blue Eyes—obviously knew who we were and wanted to talk to us about something. I strained to imagine what that might be. The only thing I could think of was something to do with Grandfather's coded notebook, but since we didn't even understand what was in it, that didn't narrow the subject matter down much, although we *were* heading roughly in the direction of location number five. A thought began to form. Maybe these guys were Russian, and Blue Eyes was old enough to have known Grandfather in 1966. Gorky sounded like a Russian name.

I took a chance and broke the silence. "Do you know Gorky?" I asked Blue Eyes.

He swung around in his seat and waved an arm to indicate to Scarface that this topic of conversation was okay. "Of course I know Gorky," he said. "I am Russian. You know Gorky?"

"I've heard of him," I replied.

Blue Eyes nodded. "And what is your favorite of his?"

"What?" The question made no sense.

"Your favorite. Mine is *The Lower Depths*, although it may not to be to your Canadian taste. It is very Russian. Perhaps his short tales are more to your liking?"

"Short tales?" I mumbled in utter confusion.

Blue Eyes looked puzzled. "You talk of our great writer, Maxim Gorky, yes? The friend of Lenin who was murdered on the orders of Stalin in 1936?"

I realized that we were talking about completely different things. I backtracked. "His short stories, yes. I have only read a few. I would like to read more."

This seemed to satisfy Blue Eyes, who smiled and turned back to the front. Laia looked at me with a puzzled expression. I shrugged. Either Blue Eyes knew nothing about the Gorky in Grandfather's notebook, or he was a wonderful actor. I sat in silence, wondering what was coming next, as the car climbed into the hills.

"Why did you bring us here?" Laia demanded. The suv had finally stopped, at the end of a dirt track on a barren hillside overlooking Palomares.

"As I said, to have conversation," Blue Eyes explained as we climbed out of the vehicle and moved a few steps away. Scarface and Tattoo Head hovered nearby. "And to appreciate the magnificent view." Blue Eyes waved an arm at the ribbon of development that marked the boundary between the land and the sea. In some places, construction sites showed where the development was creeping inland.

"These hills are honeycombed with ancient mines that once provided the wealth for Carthage, Europe's first business empire," Blue Eyes mused. "The Romans mined here as well, but since then…nothing. A few villages of scrub farmers and fishermen. Now look at what we have achieved. Is this not a miracle of human endeavor?"

"I suppose so," I said.

"You do not think so, but it is, and it has done much good. Old people who do not wish to live in cold places like my homeland now live here in the sun all year. Families may escape the drudgery of their lives for a couple of weeks of sun, sand and nightlife. Those are worthy goals, do you not think?"

I grunted noncommittally.

"Well," Blue Eyes said, apparently not bothered by my lack of agreement, "whatever one thinks, it has happened, and it is still happening. There is no more cheap land by the beach, and yet people still desire to come here. That is what you call a bottleneck. But the bottle is breaking. As you see, the buildings are crawling inland."

I nodded, but I really didn't have a clue what he was talking about or what it had to do with Grandfather or being kidnapped.

"What does that have to do with us?" I asked.

"Ah, the impatience of youth. I come from a very flexible family. We have found it a good way to survive. Many generations ago, we were poor peasants, scratching a pitiful existence from the soil of Mother Russia. Over the years we pulled ourselves up to become officials in St. Petersburg, in service of the Czars. When change came in 1917, we changed as well. We became bureaucrats for Lenin and Stalin, indispensible cogs in the wheels of Communism."

Laia sighed theatrically and looked bored. Blue Eyes ignored her and continued. "When things changed again, we embraced Capitalism and became businessmen. Do you see that point there?" He motioned to where the coast swung out to the south of us. Neither Laia nor I answered. "And that marina there?" He pointed north. "I own—how much of that?" He turned to his henchmen.

"Very near eighty percent," Scarface said in a voice that sounded as if he had swallowed gravel.

"Almost eighty percent of the properties between those two points," Blue Eyes said wistfully. "Not all in my name, of course. I control many different and diverse businesses, but it is mine nonetheless." He stopped to silently admire what he was showing us. If what he said was true, it was impressive. Owning 80 percent of the properties on several kilometers of extremely valuable coastline made Blue Eyes an extraordinarily wealthy man.

"So, you are rich," Laia said. "Why should I care?"

"You are very passionate in your opinions, Laia," Blue Eyes said, "but there are times you should reflect more. I think Felip would know by now where I am going with this."

"What does my father have to do with this?"

I heard an edge of worry in her voice.

"As we have this companionable discussion up here," Blue Eyes went on, "down there, Felip is, at this very minute, discussing the sale of a large piece of land with the American—my land."

"Your land?"

"It is land no one wants. For a few reasonable payments to the right people in the right places, and as soon as the land is declared free of contamination, I shall have first refusal on its purchase."

"Bribes, you mean," Laia said.

Blue Eyes tilted his head. "If you wish to use such crude terminology. I prefer to think of it as the lubricant for the wheels of business. In any case, the people to whom I have made payments will ensure that any paperwork Felip and the American put through will be misplaced or found to be incomplete. The American will not build in Palomares. I do not wish to have American interests on my doorstep, but discouraging them could be a long, tedious and expensive process. This way, if the American drops his interest now, things will run much more smoothly.

The land will be declared safe in the near future, and then I shall be free to build."

"And you will become even richer." Laia's voice was filled with scorn.

Blue Eyes nodded acknowledgment. "It will be good for everyone—the old people, the holiday-makers and the locals who will have work on my building sites and in the hotels, bars and nightclubs I shall build."

"And I am supposed to do what about this?" Laia asked, sounding less confident.

"I wish for you to have a conversation with your father. I would very much like you to persuade him that this venture is not in his—or anyone else's—best interests."

"He won't listen to me," Laia said, "and even if he did, why should I do this for you?"

I heard a loud click beside my right ear and turned to find myself staring down the barrel of a large pistol.

ELEVEN

Scarface had moved forward so silently, I had heard nothing, and now he was holding a gun to my head. And smiling. I instantly broke out in a cold sweat. I couldn't take my eyes off the round black hole in the center of the gun's barrel. It wasn't very large, but all I could think of was the bullet exploding out of it and tearing through the flesh and bone of my head.

"What are you doing?" There was a definite note of panic in Laia's voice now. My breath was coming in short gasps, and my mouth felt drier than the rocks and sand around us.

"I am making a point," Blue Eyes said conversationally. "You undoubtedly noticed how easily my colleagues and I picked you off the street. Please do not doubt that we can do that anytime we wish—here, in Seville or in Barcelona. I have many contacts around the world, even in Toronto—Mississauga, to be precise, Steve."

Blue Eyes smiled at me, and I swallowed hard.

"I am absolutely certain, Laia, that you would wish nothing bad to happen to Steve. I, too, would deeply regret any harm that came to him. However, the unfortunate truth is that Steve is surplus to my requirements. It is you, not your Canadian friend, who can persuade Felip to terminate the deal he is discussing with the American." He turned to Scarface. "I think Steve has seen enough of the gun."

The big man lowered his weapon, replaced it in the holster under his jacket and stepped back. He looked almost disappointed.

"I am a generous man," Blue Eyes continued. "I will give you forty-eight hours. By that time, the American must be gone and you and Felip must be on your way back to Seville." Blue Eyes nodded, and Scarface and Tattoo Head drifted toward the SUV.

"I have enjoyed our conversation," he said, turning back to Laia and me, "but I am a busy man, and my affairs do not run themselves. I regret that I cannot offer you a ride back into town, but the walk is all downhill, and it will give you a chance to reflect on my proposal." Blue Eyes smiled broadly and strolled over to the SUV. Tattoo Head opened the front passenger door for him. When the door closed, Tattoo Head looked over at us and gave a small wave. It was not a friendly gesture.

I held it together until the SUV was out of sight and then my legs gave way, and I collapsed onto my knees. Laia was crouched beside me in an instant. "Are you okay?" she asked.

I took a deep breath and let it out. "To be honest, I've been better," I said with a weak smile. "I really thought he was going to shoot me." I was almost crying with relief. Laia hugged me for a long time. When my emotions had settled down, I kissed her, and then we stood up. "What do we do now?" I asked.

"We'd better walk into town," Laia said. I glanced at my watch and was amazed how little time had passed since the SUV had picked us up. It had seemed like a lifetime.

"We should still be on time to meet Felip," Laia said.

"Do you think Felip will do what Blue Eyes wants?" I asked as we set off.

"Blue Eyes?"

"That's how I think of the old guy," I explained. "Like the singer Frank Sinatra, although I doubt our Blue Eyes has ever sung in Las Vegas."

"Didn't this Frank Sinatra have connections to organized crime?" Laia asked.

"Yeah," I said, "but I don't think anything was ever proven. Is our Blue Eyes organized crime?"

"Russian Mafia, I would guess," Laia said. "They're big players all up and down this coast now."

"He doesn't look like a mob guy."

"They all look like businessmen these days, but his friends looked like mobsters."

"You're right," I acknowledged. "Scarface and Tattoo Head."

Laia laughed. It sounded good. "Do you give everyone nicknames?"

"Not everyone," I said. "Just rude mobsters who don't introduce themselves. So Blue Eyes controls the real estate around here."

"Probably through bribes and threats," Laia explained, "but it's not only real estate. The Russians control most of the prostitution and drugs along the coast. It's easy to bring girls from Eastern Europe and hashish, cocaine and heroin from Africa and Asia into any of the ports along here. Most of the drugs in Europe come in through Mediterranean ports. It's a huge business, and people like Blue Eyes control it."

"And he doesn't want the Americans taking his business away."

"Exactly. American mobs might want to muscle in on his turf, or honest businessmen might take offense at the way he does business here. The last thing he wants is the American war-on-drugs guys sniffing around his operation."

"Do you think you'll be able to persuade Felip to back off?" I asked.

"I don't know. Felip hates to feel like he's being pressured to do something he doesn't want to. He's very stubborn. It'll depend how it's presented to him."

"How will you do that?"

"The first thing is to find out how it went with your friend Chad. If he doesn't want to go ahead, then our problem's solved."

"I hope it works out," I said, uncomfortable that my future safety might depend on Chad. "When they picked us up, I was sure it had something to do with Grandfather's notebook and the code."

"Me too. I guess we've become a bit paranoid about spies and saboteurs." Laia stopped and pulled the GPS out of her pocket.

"We don't need that," I said. "We can just follow the track down the hill."

Laia nodded and busied herself with the buttons. "I thought so," she said. "Location number five is close, just around that hillside." She pointed to the left.

"You still want to find out what Grandfather's notebook means, even after what just happened to us?"

"We can't change what happened, and we have time before we meet Felip. There's probably nothing there, but don't you want to find out for sure? If we don't find anything, then it's over. I can't think of any other leads we can follow."

"Okay," I agreed. "Let's take a quick look. I *do* want to know what the fifth location is."

We left the path and worked our way around the hillside, Laia consulting the GPS. After about ten minutes, we came to a flatter area. "We're here," Laia announced.

"You were right," I said, sitting on a large, flat rock. "There's nothing here. The ground looks the same as everywhere else in these hills—rocks, sand, cactus and a few scrub bushes. We could be on the set for a cowboy movie in New Mexico or Arizona. If anything happened here in 1966, there's no sign of it now."

"Maybe," Laia said. She was staring past me at the gently sloping hillside above us. "Some of the hillside has slumped down."

I stood up and turned around. If I looked hard, I could just make out a shallow, V-shaped groove on the hillside that led down to a jumble of rocks and dirt where the ground leveled out. The scar on the hillside, and even the rocks at its base, were barely visible. Bushes and cacti grew all over. "I see it," I said, "but this happened hundreds of years ago, maybe even when the Carthaginians or Romans were here. In any case, way before 1966."

"It did," Laia agreed, "but what do you call what's at the bottom of the slump?"

Suddenly it became clear. "A rockfall!"

"Was your grandfather telling whoever decoded the notebook that something dangerous was hidden behind the rockfall here?"

"Maybe," I said as I moved toward the rocks, "but if the slump happened long before 1966, it couldn't be the fifth bomb. This is a dead end." I was suddenly very tired and thirsty, and every time I let my mind wander, Scarface, Tattoo Head and Blue Eyes leaped into it. I sat down. "These rocks haven't moved in ages." I looked out over Palomares and the new buildings lining the coast. All owned by Blue Eyes. I had much more urgent issues than figuring out what Grandfather's cryptic notes meant. The image of the black barrel of Scarface's gun hovered before me. It made my stomach lurch, and a wave of nausea passed over me. I suddenly felt cold.

"There are marks on the rock here," Laia said from behind me. She was crouched beside it, peering at something. "There's a cross and a line and something that looks like an arrowhead."

"So what?" I asked miserably. "We're not going to find anything here. There's no magic door that will open and give us the answer to everything." I was speaking more harshly than I intended, but I was feeling sick and scared. "Can we go? I'm not feeling very well."

Immediately, Laia was beside me, the rocks forgotten. "Are you all right?" she asked.

"I don't know. My stomach doesn't feel right, and I can't get the image of Scarface holding the gun to my head out of my mind. It's probably just the tension, but can we go and see Felip? I'll feel much better if he tells us that Chad doesn't want the land and is on his way back to Madrid. Maybe we can come back and look around here later."

Laia put her hand on my forehead. "You feel clammy," she said. "Are you okay to walk down?"

"Yeah," I said. "I'll be doing something. That will help take my mind off Blue Eyes and his threats."

"Okay," Laia said, offering me her arm as I stood up shakily, "let's head down. You're probably getting dehydrated as well. Something to drink and a snack will help."

"Don't you feel scared?" I asked as we headed back to the path and down toward the town.

"Of course I do," Laia said. "I'll probably wake up in the middle of the night worrying. But while there's something that needs to be done, I can focus on that, and right now what needs to be done is getting you down the hill."

I smiled to myself, thinking, despite everything, how incredibly lucky I was to have met Laia. I began to feel better as we walked. Laia told me stories about Carthage and Rome and the wars they had fought. Her enthusiasm for her country's rich history helped lift my spirits. All I needed was something to drink and good news from Felip.

TWELVE

Any hopes I had of Chad losing interest in Palomares real estate and going home were dashed the instant Laia and I walked through the door of Pedro's. Not only had Chad not gone home, but there he was, sitting at a table with Felip, laughing and drinking wine. Laia and I exchanged glances, ordered a lemon Kas each and joined them.

"Hey, kids," Chad said cheerfully. "You have a good afternoon?"

"Yeah," I said noncommittally. "Did you find any hot properties?" I hadn't meant it as a joke, but Laia almost choked on her drink with laughter, and Felip flashed me a warning look.

Chad seemed oblivious to any double meaning. "Sure did. I know that land doesn't look like much now, but after it's cleaned up, it'll have a lot of potential. Not too far from the beach or the town, and there'll be some spectacular views from the fourteenth or fifteenth floors. You got to remember the basic rule of real estate around here: as the population ages, more and more people are going to search for the good life hereabouts, and boy, the good Lord ain't makin' any more land fer us all." Chad chuckled at his little comment and fake southern drawl.

I cringed. Chad was annoying in all his guises: cheerful joker, dull investment counselor and sleazy real-estate investor. It was difficult to tell which was the real Chad.

"So you think American businessmen will be interested in building here?" I asked.

"Sure will. Me and Felip were just thrashing out some details on how we are going to present it to them. The folks I've been talking with want to build a theme resort, and I've been thinking Roman—plenty of pillars, statues and courtyards. There'd be mosaics on the floors, and the floor numbers would be in Roman numerals. That way thirteen would be XIII and no one would get superstitious about it." Chad chuckled again.

"Is it easy for American interests to buy land in Spain and develop it?" Laia asked. "Aren't there local interests who might not be happy?"

For a moment, a serious look flashed across Chad's face, but then it was replaced by his usual toothy grin. "Oh, I reckon some folks' noses will be put out of joint, but we live in a global economy. Money's got to move where the opportunities are. That way everyone benefits. Right, Felip?"

Felip looked distinctly uncomfortable, but he just nodded.

Chad kept going. "Anyway, I was just saying to Felip that I've got a generous expense account for this trip, and I'd hate to waste it. Must be some good restaurants in those hotels by the beach. Would you kids care to join Felip and me for some dinner?"

I looked at Laia and could tell immediately that she wasn't any more keen on an evening with Chad than I was. "Thank you," I said, "but I'm not feeling so good. Probably something I ate. It'd be a shame to waste a good meal."

"And I'm sure you have more business to talk to Felip about," Laia added. "We'll just relax and maybe catch something to eat if Steve feels better later."

"Good idea," Felip said, in a tone that suggested he was happy we were not taking Chad up on his offer. "Chad has booked us into the Puesta del Sol Hotel just south of town. We checked in and dropped the bags off earlier. All you have to do is pick up keys at the desk whenever you want."

"Thanks," Laia said. "I think, if Steve feels up to it, we'll wander up and check out where bomb number two landed."

"A walk in the fresh air might do me good," I said as we stood up.

"That reminds me," Felip said. "Can I have my GPS back? I've loaded the land designations on it, and it'll help our discussions."

Laia hesitated. "You won't need it to find bomb site two," Felip said. "Just follow the main street through town. When you come out the other side, keep going until you come to the cemetery and a couple of small reservoirs. The fenced-off area is where the bomb landed."

Laia produced the GPS and handed it over.

"Kind of funny, a bomb landing by a cemetery," Chad said. No one laughed. "Anyway," he went on, "from the cemetery, go down to the main road along the coast and head south. The Puesta del Sol's signposted on the left. There's even a sign in English. *Puesta del sol* means sunset. You can't miss it." Chad laughed again, but no one else had any idea what was funny.

"It's only a couple of kilometers," Felip said, "but catch a cab if you get tired. And take some water."

"Okay," Laia said. "See you later."

"You didn't mention what happened on the hill," I said as soon as we were out on the street.

"I need to think about how best to tell Felip," Laia explained as we walked through town. "If I start off talking about gangsters, Felip will overreact, and the last thing we want right now is the police involved. It's only our word against Blue Eyes's, and he's obviously an influential person around here. Besides, I really didn't want to say anything in front of Chad."

"He's not exactly the caring, sensitive type," I said. "Let's go and look at where bomb two landed and then we can head down to the hotel. I'll probably feel like eating something by then."

"Are you okay for walking all that way?"

"Sure. I'm feeling better. Something to drink really helped. I played it up in there to get us out of dinner with Chad."

"Yeah. That wouldn't have been fun." Laia glanced at her watch. "We'll probably get back to the hotel about half past six. It'll be getting dark by then, and it'll be a good time to have a shower and grab something to eat."

"Aaaahhh," I said, taking a deep breath. "Don't you just love the energizing smell of plutonium in the evening air?" We were standing by a high chain-link fence that encircled a large area of hilly ground where bomb number two had landed and exploded. Behind us, the narrow dirt road wound back to town between two reservoirs and the local cemetery.

Laia laughed and punched me on the shoulder. "You're an idiot."

"Yes," I agreed, "but I'm a happy, harmless idiot."

"Are you happy?" Laia was suddenly serious.

"You mean despite being forced to hang out with Chad, having a mystery that seems unsolvable and being threatened by armed mobsters?" Laia smiled, but I could see she was still serious. "Yes. I'm very happy," I said, putting my arm around her shoulder. "I'm so glad you invited me here for Christmas."

"And I am glad you came," Laia said. She moved in and hugged me. "I'm very happy too," she whispered in my ear.

I could have stood there forever, on a dirt road on a warm Spanish evening with Laia's arms around me, but the peace was broken by the distant rumble of a scooter. We pulled apart.

"Do you have scooters in Canada?" Laia asked.

"Not many," I said. "I think it's mostly a European thing."

"Then perhaps I will come to Canada. It sounds like a peaceful place. Nothing ever happens there."

"That's not fair," I said with mock indignity. "Lots of stuff happens in Canada. We had the War of 1812 and the Mackenzie-Papineau Rebellion in 1837..."

"I'm sorry," Laia said. "Since 1812, we in Spain have only had a war against Napoleon, two civil wars, a lost Empire, forty years of a Fascist dictatorship, Basque terrorism, and countless rebellions."

I laughed. "One of our prime ministers said that Europe's problem was too much history."

"He was right."

"He also said that Canada suffered from too much geography."

Laia laughed. "Then I will come over in the summer and you can show me some of Canada's geography."

"I would love that," I said as a bright red scooter appeared around the corner between the reservoirs. The rider was young and helmetless, with a green scarf wrapped around the lower half of his face. He slowed as he drew level with us. I raised my hand in greeting. He ignored it and continued past, staring hard at us as he did. Once he was past, he accelerated down the hill.

"Friendly," I commented as his dust cloud drifted over us. Then a thought struck me. "Do you think Blue Eyes sent him to keep an eye on us?"

Laia shook her head and brushed the dust off her clothes. "There are many kids on scooters, especially along the coast. He probably slowed down to see if we had a bag he could easily snatch. It happens a lot, although mostly in the summer. But we should be moving on. It'll be dark soon, and I need a shower now more than ever."

As we set off down the road, Laia said, "Now, except for where bomb number four fell out to sea, we have visited all of the locations in your grandfather's notebook. What have they told us?"

"Nothing," I said. "Apart from some fences and warning signs, there's nothing to see where the bombs fell, and location five was a bust."

"There was the rockfall," Laia pointed out.

"A really old rockfall," I said.

"And the scratch marks I found."

"I bet they were really old as well. Probably some bored Roman miner writing something rude about his boss."

Laia laughed. Then she stopped so suddenly that I'd taken a couple of steps before I realized she wasn't beside me anymore. I turned to see her staring at me. "That's it!" she said.

"What?"

"Chad gave us the answer."

"Chad?" I had trouble imagining Chad having the answer to anything.

"The marks I saw on the rockfall were a cross, a line and what I thought was an arrowhead."

"Okay," I said. "What does Chad have to do with that?"

"The resort his investors are planning will have a Roman theme. Roman numerals for the floors in the hotel. XIII for thirteen." Laia crouched and scratched marks in the dust—XIV.

"It wasn't a cross, a line and an arrowhead," I said. "It was the Roman numerals for fourteen. Grandfather's code—rockfall fourteen—wasn't for rockfall number fourteen, it was number fourteen *on* a rockfall at location number five. Did you try to move the rock?"

"No. It was big, and it looked like it had been there forever. Do you think whatever is hidden from Gorky is behind that rock?"

"I'm certain of it. We need to go back there."

"It's too late now." Laia looked up to where the sun was almost touching the tops of the western hills. "It'll be pitch-dark long before we get there. We'll go tomorrow."

"Okay," I agreed. Could we be this close to solving the mystery? I was thrilled by the possibility. We had made incredible progress since this morning, even if

we weren't any closer to discovering who the saboteur at Morón Air Base was. On the other hand, this
morning I had never met Blue Eyes, Scarface or Tattoo
Head, and my life had been much simpler. I glanced
at Laia walking beside me, deep in thought. At least I
wasn't alone. I decided there was nothing I could do
about Grandfather's mystery or Blue Eyes's threats
before tomorrow anyway, so I would try my hardest
to enjoy the evening with Laia in what I was certain
would be a very expensive hotel. I was right about it
being expensive, but the Puesta del Sol Hotel turned
out to be surprising in a completely different way.

THIRTEEN

Appropriately, it was sunset when we arrived at the Puesta del Sol. There was a couple registering in front of us, so while Laia waited, I crossed the lobby to check out the pool. At the door marked *PISCINA*, a uniformed porter stepped in front of me and said, "*Usted no puede entrar en la piscina vestida de esa manera.*"

"*Perdon?*" I said.

"*Su ropa,*" the man said, indicating my clothes. "*Usted no puede entrar en la piscine.*"

"Okay," I said, turning away. I knew I was dusty and could use a shower, and my clothes weren't from

Chad's tailor, but I was a little annoyed that the hotel was so pompous that I wouldn't be allowed into the pool area. I looked around the echoing lobby. It was certainly upscale—not at all like the motels Mom, DJ and I stayed in when we went on holidays. The floor was of gleaming marble, the walls either glass or polished wood, and there were crystal chandeliers and plush seats all around. Even the row of elevator doors was polished to a mirror finish.

As I watched, one set of elevator doors opened and a dumpy, middle-aged couple came out. They were chatting happily, and both had white towels over their shoulders. There was nothing remarkable about them—a couple going for a swim before dinner and the evening's entertainment—except that both were completely naked.

I watched in shocked confusion as they crossed the lobby, smiling and nodding at me on the way, exchanged a couple of friendly words with the porter and disappeared through the doors to the pool. My clothes weren't the best or the cleanest, but at least they were clothes.

I spun around toward the registration desk and collided with another naked person. "Watch where you're going," he said in English. I mumbled some kind of apology and kept going. Laia was at the desk, talking to the receptionist. "There are naked people here," I blurted out.

Laia looked startled, but the receptionist simply said, "Of course there are, sir. The Puesta del Sol Hotel is a naturist resort. Clothing is optional in most areas, although clothes are not allowed in the pool area and are essential at all times in the restaurant and after eight in the evening everywhere." I could think of nothing to say. "I'm sorry," the receptionist went on. "You were not aware of this fact?"

"A simple misunderstanding," Laia said. She seemed remarkably calm. "My friend Steve is from Canada. I don't think they have many naturist resorts there. Perhaps it is too cold."

The receptionist smiled. "I think you will be more comfortable after eight o'clock," she said to me. "I hope you enjoy your stay with us." I glanced at the clock on the wall behind her. An hour and a half until people put their clothes on.

"I've got our room keys," Laia said. "You are in four twelve and I am in four thirteen; our bags are already there. Perhaps we should go up, shower and relax.

I'll meet you back here at five minutes past eight." She exchanged a smile with the receptionist.

Laia led me over to the elevator. I kept my eyes firmly on a small patch of the marble floor in front of me. When the doors were safely closed, I looked up. "Did you know this?" I asked.

"No," Laia said, "but there are many naturist resorts along the coast. Sofia and Felip used to bring me on holiday to them when I was young."

"Are you a naturist?" I asked.

"No," she said to my great relief. "It is not for me, but if you do want to take your clothes off, the south of Spain is probably a good place to do it."

"If you have lots of sunscreen," I said.

Laia laughed. "You see, already you are getting used to it." The elevator doors opened and we pushed out past a large, noisy, naked family on their way to the pool. At the door of 412, we stopped. "Don't worry," Laia said. "No one has to take their clothes off—unless they want to go for a swim. I'll see you downstairs—after eight. It's been an exciting day." She smiled, kissed me on the cheek and went on to room 413. I fumbled with my key card, fell into the room, closed the door and collapsed on the bed beside my backpack. I wasn't sure how much more excitement I could take.

"Do you feel more comfortable now?" Laia and I were looking at each other across a spotless white tablecloth in the largest restaurant I'd ever been in. It was 8:15, early to be eating dinner in Spain, so the restaurant was quiet. The few diners there were all fully clothed.

"I think I've gotten over the shock," I said. "You know what I first thought when I saw the naked couple come out of the elevator? It was a line from *The Sixth Sense*."

"The scary ghost movie about the kid who says, 'I see dead people'?"

"Yeah. My first thought was, 'I see naked people.'" Laia laughed. "The rooms are great though," I went on. "The bed's so soft, I fell asleep as soon as I lay down. I only woke up half an hour ago, but a shower and clean clothes made me feel like a new person."

"That's a shame," Laia said. "I liked the old person. But the rooms *are* nice. I sat on the balcony for a while, looking out over the pool and the palm trees to the lights of the boats out at sea. I suppose some people live like this all the time."

"I feel more relaxed than I have all day. Shall we eat?"

Dinner was a buffet that stretched the full length of the restaurant. There was food from all over Europe, but Laia insisted we eat local dishes. I had shrimp, octopus, fried local fish, ham, salad and a wonderful pastry dessert dripping in honey. I returned to the buffet three times.

"You won't need to eat for the rest of your holiday," Laia commented after I had finally finished and sat back in my chair.

"I'm not so sure about that, but I'm certainly eating well. Almost enough to fuel all the walking we're doing."

"And there'll be more tomorrow," Laia said, "if we're going to walk back up to location number five."

"What does Felip have planned for tomorrow?"

"I don't know. I suspect there will be a lot of legal paperwork he will need to check on so that Chad can be fully informed when he goes back to whoever's behind this scheme. He'll probably have to drive down to Almería."

Mention of Chad brought back memories of Scarface and Blue Eyes's threat. "By tomorrow, we'll be halfway through the forty-eight hours," I pointed out.

"I know," Laia said. "If we see Felip tonight, I'll try and find out what's going on. If Chad's not *too* keen, finding out about the laws and regulations he'll have to get around might be enough to discourage him. If not, I'll tell Felip about Blue Eyes tomorrow night."

I must have looked worried, because Laia went on, "It will be all right. If all else fails, we'll be gone from here before the forty-eight hours are up anyway. Blue Eyes's threats were meant to scare us. It makes no sense for him to chase us to Barcelona or Canada. He would just be increasing his risk, and there would be nothing to gain by it. It's not rational."

"I'm not convinced that Blue Eyes is entirely rational," I said. "He's a Russian mobster, after all."

"But that's what makes him rational. He wants to be able to carry out his illegal activities with a minimum of fuss and without drawing unwelcome attention. He's not above threatening people or hurting them if necessary, but he wants to maintain at least the façade of being a reputable businessman.

There has to be a gain to outweigh any risk he runs, and there's no gain in chasing either of us."

"I suppose so." What Laia said made sense, but I'd still be much happier with Chad gone and all talk of building Roman-style resorts ended.

"Hello, you two." We looked up to see Felip coming toward us. I was relieved to see he was alone.

"Hello," Laia said. "I wasn't expecting you here so early. Where's Chad?"

"He said he had people to see," Felip said, sitting down beside us. "To be honest, I find him a bit…"

"Tiring?" I suggested.

Felip nodded. "He is cheerful all the time. Everything is so positive. I'm afraid I find it a bit wearing."

"I know what you mean," I said. "Do you think he will go ahead with this Roman resort project?"

"I don't know. He goes on about how wonderful the idea is, but the decision's not up to him. He's simply checking things out for an American company."

"What will the local businesses think of an American company moving in?" Laia asked.

"Good question," Felip said. "As you can see from all the building along the coast, there's a lot of investment here already. Much of it's foreign money."

"Russian?" I asked.

"Some," Felip said. "It's hard to tell where the money comes from, and there are many different companies that could easily all be owned by one man. But there is a strong Russian connection. This resort, for instance, is owned by a company called Gorky Holdings, which certainly suggests a Russian connection."

Laia and I exchanged looks at the mention of Gorky. It was a name that seemed to crop up everywhere.

"What do you think of the resort?" Felip asked with a smile.

"You mean apart from the naked people all over the place?" I said, smiling back. "That was a shock at first, but the resort seems fine. I'm not sure I'll use the pool though."

"There are a lot of naturist resorts along this stretch of coast. Chad said he booked us in here because it was the only place with space that was close to Palomares. Otherwise, we would have had to drive in from Almería. Speaking of which, I have to go down there tomorrow to look at land-titles records and talk to people. What are your plans?"

"I think we'll walk up into the hills and look at location number five," Laia said. "I doubt if there's anything to see, but I'll bet the views are spectacular up there."

"They are," Felip said. "Take plenty of water with you. I should be back in the afternoon. I have to meet with Chad, but we can have dinner later. Perhaps the next day we can drive north and poke around the ruins in Cartagena?" Felip stood up. "I have paperwork and emails to catch up on, so I'm going to head on up. See you down here for breakfast?"

"Sounds good," I said as Laia and I also stood. "Good night."

"Good night," Laia added.

When Felip had gone, we signed the meal bills to our rooms. "Let's get a breath of fresh air," Laia suggested. We strolled through the lobby, nodded to the doorman and headed outside. The air had cooled since midafternoon, but it was still pleasantly warm. We wandered up the drive toward the road, without any specific goal. "I guess Blue Eyes does own this place then," Laia said. "He certainly seemed to be into Gorky."

"Yeah," I agreed. "Do you think he might be the Gorky in Grandfather's notebook? He might be old enough."

"He could be, but when you asked him if he knew Gorky, he talked about someone else."

"I suppose so. We may never solve that part of the mystery." I stopped and pointed to a red scooter under one of the streetlights. "Isn't that the scooter that passed us on the road this afternoon?"

"There are a lot of scooters around," she said, "and I don't think the kid we saw could afford to stay in this place."

"Hi, kids!" A figure stepped out of the shadows. I couldn't see who it was, but I would recognize that cheerful voice anywhere. Laia groaned audibly as Chad strode toward us. "You two going for a romantic evening stroll?"

"Yeah, something like that," I said. "I thought you had a meeting."

"All done," Chad said. "You've got to be quick in this business. You snooze, you lose."

I was tempted to keep walking, but I had a question I wanted to ask. "Do you think your American investors will go ahead with the Roman resort project?"

"It's a wonderful investment opportunity," Chad enthused. "In the long term, it can't fail, and the cleanup costs will be absorbed quickly. I think they'd be crazy not to run with it."

Now it was my turn to groan. Chad gave me an odd look, part concern and part thoughtful, not like him at all. "But," he said eventually, "if you want my honest opinion, I suspect the politics will be too much for them. I think we're a few years away from any development on that land."

My heart leaped, and I had trouble not shouting out loud. "Oh," I said as noncommittally as possible.

"You kids have a good walk," Chad said, winking broadly at me. "Don't go too far. You never know what kind of people are around these days. Good night."

"Good night," I said.

Chad headed for the hotel lobby, and Laia and I continued out to the road. "I was terrified he was going to suggest he come for a walk with us," Laia said.

"Just as well he didn't," I said. "I would have had to kill him." We laughed. "I was glad to hear he doesn't think the deal will go through with his investors. Blue Eyes should be glad to hear that."

Laia nodded, and we linked arms. We strolled along the road and down to the beach, happy just to be in each other's company. When we got back, I noticed that the red scooter was still there.

FOURTEEN

Breakfast the next day was a long-drawn-out affair with Chad blabbing on about how to make money. He was interested in what Laia and I were going to do that day, and I was terrified he was going to offer to accompany us. I didn't feel comfortable telling him anything, but Felip gave him a sketchy outline of what we had found out from Grandfather's notebook. "Well," Chad had said as we eventually managed our escape, "don't you kids go finding any more nuclear bombs. It's hard enough persuading people to invest here as it is."

With a huge sigh of relief, we wished Felip a good trip to Almería, arranged to meet him that evening for dinner and then escaped both Chad and the naked people who were beginning to show up throughout the hotel. "We need to pick up some bottles of water," Laia said as we headed into town. "It's going to be a hot day."

I glanced up at the clear blue sky which, even in midmorning, was already painfully bright. "I'll pick up a pair of shades as well," I said. "I never thought to bring mine. They're not something I use much in Toronto in December."

"A flashlight might help as well," Laia added. "In case we do manage to move that rock."

"Good idea." I was about to comment on how glad I was that Chad hadn't offered to keep us company when the red scooter shot past us. The rider was wearing a green scarf again, even though there was no dust on the main road. "That's the same guy we saw yesterday—I'm sure of it," I said. "Do you think he's following us?"

"Why would he do that?"

"I don't know," I admitted. "I guess I'm feeling a bit paranoid what with Grandfather's secret codes and Blue Eyes's threats."

"Palomares is a small town," Laia explained. "He probably works the night shift at the hotel and passed us on his way to work yesterday. Now he's heading home."

"Probably," I said. It made sense. We found a store and bought water, sunglasses, snacks for the day and a cheap flashlight. "We forgot to get the GPS from your dad," I said.

"We won't need it. The rockfall will be easy enough to find."

That was true—we just needed to follow the track we had come down the day before—but I would have felt more comfortable with the GPS. That was silly, I told myself. If we didn't do anything stupid, like wandering off into the hills, we would be fine. I was beginning to worry about every little thing. I hadn't been able to fall asleep the night before, worrying about DJ and whether he was getting into a situation he couldn't handle. That was really dumb, since DJ could take care of himself and I was the one who had been threatened by the Russian Mafia. Still, I had texted him, asking how he was doing, before switching off my phone and finally falling asleep.

I pushed my worries aside and determined to enjoy the day with Laia, but as we turned off the main road and onto the track into the hills, I looked back and caught a glimpse of a red scooter stopped by the side of the road, the guy in the scarf crouched beside it.

It was lunchtime when we reached our destination. We took a moment to sit on the flat rock, drink some water, eat a snack and enjoy the magnificent view of the sparkling Mediterranean. Then we examined the rockfall carefully.

"No other marks on any of the rocks," I said.

"True," Laia said, "but there's a lot of lichen and dirt on many of the rocks. It would take a lot more time than we have to check thoroughly."

"I guess we should try and move number fourteen."

At first, it didn't seem as if the rock was going to move, but with some scraping around the edges and by rocking it back and forth, we managed to loosen it. Eventually, it came free and rolled to one side. For a moment, Laia and I just stood there, breathing heavily and staring at the dark hole we had revealed.

"I feel like Howard Carter when he discovered Tutankhamen's tomb," I said.

"Well, I hope there're no dead bodies inside," Laia commented as she reached into her daypack for the flashlight. She switched it on, and we both leaned forward eagerly.

At first, we couldn't see much in the narrow beam. The ground seemed to slope gently down, but the hole wasn't large enough for us both to get our heads in and look around. After we had banged heads a couple of times, Laia pulled back and handed me the flashlight. "Here, you have a look around. It'll be easier for one person."

I stretched my arm into the hole, trying not to think of poisonous spiders or mummified bodies. At first I had no better luck than before, but then I caught a dull glint at the edge of the flashlight beam. By stretching as far as I could into the hole and peering hard, I could just make out what appeared to be a pale sphere. The surface was divided into hexagons, like a soccer ball.

I stared at the object for so long that Laia asked, "What do you see?"

I pulled out of the hole, scratching my shoulder and bringing down a clod of dirt that broke into choking dust. I coughed and took a drink of water while Laia fidgeted impatiently. "It's there," I said at last.

"What is?" Laia asked, although I was certain she knew what I was talking about. Felip had said the main part of the bomb was about the size of a soccer ball, and that the complex explosives designed to set it off were arranged in a pattern that resembled a honeycomb.

"The plutonium trigger bomb," I said.

We stared at each other. We had discovered one of the most powerful weapons ever built. It had to be from one of the bombs that had fallen that day in 1966, but what was it doing here? Had sabotage by someone called Gorky caused it to fall here? Had Grandfather found it? Had he hidden it? If so, why had he never told anyone about it?

"The hole's probably big enough to squeeze through," I said. "Should I go in?"

"Do you want to crawl into a hole with a plutonium bomb?" Laia asked. "It won't explode, but what if some of the plutonium has escaped? If we go kicking dust around, who knows what we'll be breathing in?"

"I don't want to go in either," I said. "Apart from anything else, the rocks above the hole don't look too stable. Even if there's no plutonium, I don't want to get trapped in an old mine, or whatever it is. What should we do?"

"We'll put the rock back," Laia said. "Then we'll go down and tell Felip what we've found. He'll know who to contact."

I nodded my agreement, glad that we had someone we could talk to. It was even harder to get the rock back in place, but we managed. We ate and drank some more and then, with the afternoon sun high above us, we set off down the hill.

"Is this the end of it?" Laia asked as we walked.

"I don't know. We've certainly done a lot more than I ever thought we could when DJ sent the note-book pages. We broke the code, worked out the locations and much of what Grandfather's cryptic comments meant—and we've discovered the missing bomb. That's pretty impressive."

"It is," Laia agreed, "but we still don't know the whys—why your grandfather came back to Spain under a false name and why he hid the bomb."

"And we don't know who Gorky is, or was, or what the saboteur had to do with everything. I keep making up stories in my head to explain it all, but nothing works. There's something we're missing. The question is whether we'll ever figure it out."

I looked at Laia walking beside me. She was as dirty and tired as me, and her shirt had a jagged rip on the left shoulder, but she was still beautiful. "You look like you've been in a war," I said.

"And you think you look as if you've just walked out of a beauty parlor?" Laia said, looking at me with a broad smile. Her brow suddenly furrowed. "Are you okay?" she asked, pointing at my shoulder.

I looked down at where I had scratched myself on the rocks around the edge of the hole. There was a dark, rapidly drying bloodstain on my T-shirt. "It's just a scratch," I said. "Maybe I'll go for a swim back at the hotel and show off my war wound."

"If you do, you're on your own," Laia said. "Your war wound is not all you'd have to show off to go for a swim."

We laughed. "I still can't believe we ended up in a naturist resort. Maybe we can get our swimsuits and go down to the beach for a swim?" I suggested.

"That sounds like a better idea. I'd certainly enjoy washing this dirt off."

We walked in silence for a while. "I know you don't think Grandfather was a traitor," I said eventually, "and I don't either, but someone obviously did, and we haven't found anything that proves he wasn't. That bothers me."

"Maybe DJ and the others have found out more."

"I texted DJ last night," I said, suddenly remembering that I hadn't turned my phone back on this morning. I took it out and turned it on.

"I've only got one bar," I said, looking at the screen. The phone pinged as it downloaded text that I'd missed. "It's from DJ," I said, holding the phone so Laia could see it.

Hope things are going well. We broke the code—sort of--and it might work for your entries as well. Frequency of letters. 1 = e, 2 = t, 3 = a, 4 = o. You get the idea. Look up the rest. Gotta sleep. Good luck.

"Sounds as if DJ's code is different from ours," I said, putting the phone back in my pocket. "I wonder if everyone got a different code."

"We were lucky you worked out that the key was Lorca's poem," Laia said. "We could still be completely in the dark."

"But there's still a lot that doesn't make sense," I said. "It looks like Grandfather was a spy, but who for? He came to Spain, but where else did he go?"

We walked on in silence, both deep in thought. I still hadn't come up with any answers when the red scooter shot around the bend ahead of us and skidded to a halt. We stopped and stared at the rider, who peered at us over his scarf. "What do you want?" I shouted, stepping forward.

The scooter engine roared, but instead of turning back down the hill, the man accelerated past us in a cloud of dust. When it settled, I looked back up the hill and saw the scooter stopped a couple hundred meters from us; the rider was talking into a cell phone.

"I don't like this," Laia said.

"Me neither. Let's get down to the main road as quick as we can." We hurried down the hill, the scooter keeping its distance behind us. I had a horrible sick feeling in the pit of my stomach, and it only got worse when a white panel van appeared on the road ahead. The van slewed sideways across the road and the doors slid open. Right then I would have been happy to see Scarface and Tattoo Head, but three men we'd never seen before jumped out and ran toward us. There was nowhere to go. I put my arms around Laia. The men grabbed us and hustled us into the van, where our hands and feet were bound and rags were tied around our eyes. The van lurched, and I rolled painfully against the side. "Are you okay?" I heard Laia shout.

"*¡Callate!*" A voice ordered us to shut up.

"I'm okay!" was all I had time to reply before someone hit me hard on the side of the head. We had been kidnapped for the second time in as many days and were helpless in the back of a strange van, going who knew where. The whole thing had taken only seconds.

FIFTEEN

The trip in the van was a nightmare. Because of the blindfolds, every bump and swerve came as a surprise. Because we couldn't brace ourselves to prepare, we were thrown around mercilessly, often crashing into each other and cursing our captors, who simply responded with kicks. In no time, the only part of me that wasn't bruised and sore was my back. Our abductors hadn't bothered to remove my daypack, and now, with my hands tied behind me, I couldn't have got it off even if I had wanted too. It afforded some protection, but my fear was worse than the pounding I was taking.

I had expected our kidnappers to take us down the hill, back toward town. Instead, the slope of the van floor and the increasingly bumpy road suggested that we were heading farther into the hills. We were totally at the mercy of these people, and the thought of moving away from civilization terrified me. Images of stopping at some remote location, being hustled out of the van, shot and buried in a shallow grave haunted me. Our bodies would never even be found—Felip, Sofia, Mom, DJ and the rest of the world would never know what had happened to us. And I had no idea why this was happening.

After what seemed like a lifetime but could have been no more than ten or fifteen minutes, the van stopped. I heard the door slide open. The binding on our feet was taken off, and we were pushed unceremoniously out of the van. "Laia?" I asked.

"I'm here," she said. Rough hands grabbed us and dragged us over bumpy ground. We were pushed against a wall. We were going to be shot. I moved sideways until my shoulder touched Laia's. "I love you," I said.

"*¡Siéntate!*" We were ordered to sit. The voice was harsh, but the order was comforting. You didn't shoot people when they were sitting down—did you?

We slid our backs down the wall until we were sitting. Footsteps receded. After a few minutes of silence, I risked speaking. "Are you all right?"

"Yes, apart from some cuts and bruises. You?"

"The same." Encouraged by the fact that no one had kicked us or ordered us to shut up, I went on. "Who are these people, and what do they want?" I was scared, but trying to work out what was happening calmed me down.

"I don't know," Laia replied. "I don't think they have anything to do with Blue Eyes. I don't think this is the way he works."

"Neither do I. The guy on the red scooter must have been following us."

"But he didn't do a very good job. He was obviously surprised to see us when he came around the corner."

"So he'd lost us," I said. "When he saw us, he got on his cell phone and called the white van up there."

"That means they were planning to kidnap us all along."

The thought didn't make me feel any happier. "So they were following us ever since we got to Palomares, just waiting for a chance to take us."

"It looks that way," Laia agreed, "but that doesn't get us any closer to knowing who they are or what they want."

I leaned closer to Laia and lowered my voice. "Do you think it has anything to do with Grandfather's notebook and what we found behind the rockfall?"

"Maybe," Laia said. "What we found is certainly valuable, but how could they possibly know about your grandfather's notebook?"

"I don't know. Maybe they want to hold us for ransom."

"Maybe," Laia said again, but she didn't sound convinced. "With all the rich tourists around here, I'm sure there are better targets than us. It could be something to do with Felip's work, either digging up the past or helping the people in Palomares get proper compensation."

"Could be," I acknowledged. None of our theories sounded convincing, but I didn't want to dwell on the other, less pleasant ideas I'd been having. "Where do you think we are?"

"We certainly headed farther into the hills," Laia said. "Judging from my bruises, the van was being driven fairly fast. Even if we were only traveling for ten minutes, we could be ten or fifteen kilometers away from where they picked us up. That means we could be almost anywhere. There are dozens of tracks cutting through these hills—old roads leading to abandoned mines and hunters' trails."

"The wall we're sitting against could be a ruined mine building," I suggested.

"Quite possibly. My blindfold lets through a bit of light, and it didn't get darker when we were brought to this wall, so if we're in a building, it has no roof."

We sat in silence for a while, and I thought over what had happened. We had been abducted by strangers for some unknown reason, bound and blindfolded, and we were being held in an abandoned building somewhere in the hills above Palomares. The only encouraging aspect was that we weren't already dead. We were waiting for something, but what?

"Did you mean what you said?" Laia asked, interrupting my thoughts.

"When?"

"When we were brought in here and pushed against the wall."

I had said I loved her. "Yes. I did mean it. I thought they were going to shoot us."

"So you love me," Laia said, a hint of laughter in her voice, "but only when you think we're about to die."

"No. I mean, yes." I took a deep breath. "I love you all the time," I said. "When I'm sleeping and awake, eating, studying for exams, on planes with boring people like Chad *and* when I think I'm about to die."

Laia leaned into me and rested her head on my shoulder. "And I love you too," she said.

Despite our situation, in that moment I was blissfully happy. But this was new emotional territory for me. What was I supposed to say next? Before I had a chance to think of anything, I heard tires crunching on gravel nearby and doors opening and closing.

"*¡Párate!*" We struggled to our feet.

"*Quite el antifaz.*" A new voice, softer than the others, was giving orders. Someone moved toward us and removed our blindfolds. The first thing I did was look at Laia. She was even grubbier and more disheveled than before, and there was a bruise forming on her cheek, but she was looking at me and smiling. I smiled back.

"Young love. How romantic." I looked at the source of the voice. We were in the remains of a square stone building, the ruined walls no more than two meters high. Across from us, in what had once been a doorway, an old man stood and stared at us. He was well-dressed and leaned on an elaborately carved walking stick. He had a full head of hair, but it was snow-white, and his face was heavily wrinkled. He only had one arm.

"I am sorry to keep you waiting," he said in heavily accented English, "but I do not get around as easily as I did in my younger days. I hope you have not been too roughly treated."

"What do you want?" I asked as confidently as I could manage.

"Ah, the impatience of youth." The man took a step into the room and said something over his shoulder. One of the men who had bundled us into the van appeared and set up a folding chair. The old man sat down and placed his stick between his knees. "We shall get to what I want in the fullness of time, but first I must tell you a story, and for that I need to sit. You shall remain standing.

"I was a twelve-year-old boy in Barcelona when the Fascist army rebelled in 1936. My parents were both Anarchists. My father was killed at the barricades in the street fighting in Barcelona in the first days of the war. My mother joined Buenaventura Durruti's militia column and was killed in the fighting for Caspe in Aragón."

Despite talking about the death of his parents, the old man spoke in a monotone, as if he were giving us a lecture on ancient history. I had no idea why he was telling us all this, but I listened intently. The shallow grave was still in the back of my mind.

"The Anarchists were brave, but they were stupid," the man went on. "They were good at street fighting, but they were a rabble. You do not defeat an army by sending poorly armed women and boys with no tanks or planes against regular soldiers with machine guns. For that you need organization and discipline. I never forgave the Anarchists for the death of my mother."

The old man fell silent, and his gazed drifted off. Laia and I waited patiently. I wondered what would happen if our storyteller died in the middle of his tale.

Would our captors let us go or kill us? Fortunately, I didn't have to find out.

"The Communists were the answer," he went on eventually. "They were organized, and their discipline was like iron. I was living on the streets, and they took me in. I lived in their barracks as a kind of mascot. During the fighting in Barcelona against the Anarchists in 1937, I was a messenger, helping keep the central authority and the fighting units in contact. I was proud to be a part of the destruction of those who had been responsible for my mother's death.

"In 1938, things were not going well for us, and I persuaded the commissar to allow me to join a unit and take part in the great attack across the Ebro River. I was assigned as a replacement to the Mackenzie-Papineau Battalion of the Fifteenth Brigade."

My head snapped around to look at Laia to see if she had picked up the reference to the unit Grandfather had fought with. She nodded and continued to stare at the old man.

"I see you have heard of that unit," he said. "It was very famous. I was honored to be a part of it and to help in the attack that would turn the tide in the war.

This was not going to be like the attack that killed my mother two years before. We were a real army, and I thought we would win. Unfortunately, we did not, and I did not get a chance to be a part of it.

"I crossed the river with the second wave on the morning of July 25th. We were organizing ourselves to continue our advance when a Fascist shell exploded on the hillside nearby. Several men were killed, but I was lucky." He waved the stump of his missing arm. "I only lost an arm."

A vague memory of something Laia and I had read in Grandfather's war journal was struggling to surface in my brain. Before it could, the old man went on. "I was in shock, of course, and disappointed that I could not be a part of the battle, but as I was being led back down the slope to the boats, I passed a young Canadian International Brigader. He was not much older than me and he looked scared, but our eyes met and the look of sympathy he gave as I passed is something I will never forget. It was only later that I learned that this young Canadian soldier was your grandfather, David McLean."

SIXTEEN

"How?" It was all I could manage to stammer. There were so many questions swirling around my head that I wasn't even sure which one I was asking. How did he know it was my grandfather? How did he know I was coming to Palomares? How did it all tie together with the coded notebook?

"You have many questions," the man said. "That is normal. All will be answered in time, but first I think we should drink." He turned to one of the younger Spaniards who had been hovering nearby. "*Agua por favor.*" The man stepped outside and returned with three bottles of cold water. He handed one to the old man.

I thought for a moment that he was going to untie our hands so we could drink, but he simply uncapped the bottles and held them to our mouths. It was messy, and much of the water splashed down my shirt front, but it tasted good.

"*Gracias*," I said before I realized I was thanking someone who had kidnapped me and quite possibly had worse in store.

"*De nada*," the man said as he walked away.

"I regret that I cannot untie you," the old man said, "but I find it is usually best to take a minimum of chances."

"Who are you?" Laia asked.

"That is a very good question. I have had many names. Perhaps I shall tell you some as a part of my story. For the moment, should you wish to be sociable, you may call me Gorky."

"Gorky!" Laia and I exclaimed. This old man sitting across from us was the mysterious man that Grandfather had hidden the bomb from. The man who must not find it because it was too dangerous.

"I see you know the name," the man said with a faint smile. "I know that you are Steve and your companion is Laia, so now that we are introduced,

I shall continue with my tale. I did not think so at the time, but I was very lucky on the banks of the Ebro that day in 1938. Had I not been wounded, I doubt I would have survived the weeks of fighting that were to come, and had I not been wounded so close to what few medical facilities we had, I would have bled to death long before a doctor saw me.

"As it was, I was ferried back across the river I had crossed with such high hopes less than an hour before. At the field hospital, a doctor cleaned the stump of my arm and tied off the severed blood vessels. I was sent back to Barcelona in an ambulance, a journey that I have little memory of, thankfully, and put in a hospital on the Ramblas to recover.

"For the first few days, I was feverish, but my arm healed well. Imagine my surprise when I became aware of my surroundings and found that I was in the bed next to the young Canadian soldier who had looked at me so sympathetically. He had made it all the way to Gandesa, as far as any of our forces made it in that battle, and had been wounded much less seriously than I. He had broken ribs and gave up his bed to a more serious case within a few days.

"He was there with a companion who had a piece of shrapnel in his shoulder, and they and a young nurse attended to my needs most generously. I think you might know who these people were?"

I nodded. The young Canadian was my grandfather, his friend was Bob (the other survivor of their group at Gandesa), and the nurse was Maria, Laia's great-grandmother. "David, Bob and Maria," Laia said under her breath.

"Exactly," Gorky said. "We became quite close, and I was sorry when David and Bob were repatriated. Maria continued to care for me, but it was a long recuperation. By the time I had recovered, the war was almost over, and I joined the flood of refugees heading for the camps in France. It was obvious that I could not return to Spain, so I prepared for a new life in France. I contacted the local Communists and, when France fell to the Nazis, took to the countryside to work for the Resistance. On one side, my lost arm was a handicap. But on the other, I could play the role of a disabled veteran, which gained me sympathy and made me seem unthreatening.

"I survived the war by good luck and spent several years drifting. I was still a young man, but what could

I do? I was disabled and had no training other than war. I could pass for a Frenchman easily enough, but I was always aware that I was far from home. I survived through odd jobs and petty crime, changing identities as it suited me.

"By the 1950s, the Cold War was at its height. I still kept in touch with other Spanish refugees and with the Communists, but did not particularly care that America was now the enemy. One evening I went to listen to a Canadian, Robert Carlyle, speak about his experiences in Spain. Imagine my surprise when it turned out to be Bob, your grandfather's friend from the hospital in Barcelona. After a few drinks and some reminiscences about the old times and what we had done with our lives since 1938, we parted.

"I never expected to see Bob again, but several months later there was a knock on the door of the seedy apartment I was living in in Marseilles. It was Bob, carrying a bottle of expensive Spanish brandy. Over the bottle, he explained how he had become disillusioned with democracy and become a dedicated Communist, working for the Soviet Union. He told me there were networks of spies and sleeper agents throughout the British and American governments, and that he was a recruiter for these networks."

"Did he mention my grandfather?" I blurted out. Ever since Gorky had mentioned meeting Grandfather, Bob and Maria in Barcelona, I had been riveted by his story, hoping that somehow it would solve the mystery of the money, passports and notebook behind the wall at the cabin.

"He did," the old man said, "but only in the vaguest sense. He gave the impression that David McLean was involved in the network that Bob was running, but without saying specifically what his role was.

"In any case, he offered me support in creating a network of Spanish refugees who could be given new identities and sent back home to spy and carry out works of sabotage. This would have the double advantage of both undermining Franco's Fascist regime and hurting the Americans, who at that time were the only ones supporting Spain, something they did in exchange for the use of Spanish air bases for nuclear bombers."

Gorky's story was long and convoluted—my shoulders ached and my hands were going numb from being tied tightly together—but what I was hearing was all beginning to fit in with what we had discovered in Grandfather's coded notebook. Both Laia and I fidgeted from foot to foot, trying to keep our blood circulating, but our full attention was on Gorky.

"I had no difficulty recruiting men and women for the tasks Bob gave me. At first we were very amateurish, and most of those sent over the mountains in the first years were captured and executed fairly quickly, but I learned, as did those who survived their first missions, that patience was the key. Instead of sending parties of saboteurs over with equipment and orders to blow up this bridge or that railway line, what we needed to do was create networks of sleepers within Spain. Dedicated men and women who survived under their false identities, did not attract attention to themselves and waited." Gorky looked at Laia. "Your great-grandmother Maria was one."

I snapped my head to the side to see Laia staring, open-mouthed, at Gorky. "Maria," she managed to gasp out eventually. "Maria was a spy? A saboteur?"

"You see," Gorky said with a smile. "Life turns out to be more complex than you assume. A saboteur? No. Maria made it very clear when I recruited her that, however much she hated the Fascists, she would do nothing to harm another human being. She accepted my offer as a way of returning to her beloved Barcelona with her young child, and agreed to undertake things that did not conflict with her strict moral code. I respected that. After all, she had nursed me through my injury, and I owed her a great deal.

"A spy? Not in the sense that you think. She did not run around stealing state secrets and putting them in drop boxes in hollow trees, or chase down the enemy like James Bond. Her undermining of the system was much more subtle. She taught and educated young women to be teachers and nurses, to care for other human beings. It was not openly political, and yet her work *was* subversive. If you teach someone to care for other human beings and to respect life, they will not become Fascists.

"The other thing that Maria did was quietly collect stories. Stories of knocks on doors in the middle of the night, stolen babies, bodies discovered at dawn by cemetery walls, the locations of forgotten graves. She knew that one day Spain would change and that remembering would become important once more. I think the work that Felip does owes much to what Maria did all those years ago.

"But I am becoming distracted, and my tale nears its end. By the mid-1960s I had an extensive network of sleepers in place across Spain, and I felt the time was right to undertake a major act of sabotage—one that would shock the world. I suggested several possibilities to Bob, but he felt the time was not right and refused to give me support. Eventually, I decided to act on my own—after all, what was the point of our work if nothing came of it?

"My prize sleeper was a young man called Arturo. He was an orphan from the war, but he was also from the Basque provinces in the north. The *Euskadi Ta Askatasuna*, or ETA, a Basque separatist group, was just beginning its campaign of violence in support of independence for the Basque country, and this made Arturo the perfect candidate. If he was captured, the Fascists would assume he was a Basque terrorist, and attention would be diverted from my organization. Also, Arturo had managed to get himself a job inside the American air base at Morón.

"Without informing Bob, I traveled to Spain under a false name and delivered a small package of explosives to Arturo. I knew that the Americans refueled their B-52 bombers in Morón, and I conceived the idea of bringing one down and, if possible, triggering a nuclear explosion in Spanish skies. Such an event would be the perfect gesture. It would shock the world, discredit Franco's regime and force the Americans to remove their already unpopular air bases in Europe."

I stared at the wrinkled old man sitting across from me. He was talking in a monotone about an act that could have killed thousands of people, turned vast areas into a radioactive wasteland and quite possibly triggered a world war. Laia and I exchanged horrified looks.

"You're insane!" I said. "You might have destroyed the world."

The old man laughed, a dry, bitter sound. "It is not I who is insane," he said. "It is the world that you seem to think so highly of. A world that destroyed my childhood, took my arm and left me with nothing. What do I owe this world?"

SEVENTEEN

So the explosion over Palomares had been sabotage, Arturo was the saboteur at the air base, and Gorky was his controller. It all fit, but where was Grandfather in all this?

"Think of the effect had one or all of those bombs exploded." Gorky was staring up at the empty sky, an almost wistful tone in his voice. "Each bomb was seventy times as powerful as the bomb that obliterated Hiroshima in 1945. Think if all four had exploded that morning." Gorky was old and frail, but his eyes gleamed with an unnatural light as he thought of the devastation that might have been wrought in the skies over Palomares. "Then the world would have had to pay attention to us."

Gorky blinked rapidly and calmed down. "I was a fool," he went on. "In those days, I had no idea how hard it is to trigger a nuclear explosion. Without the bombs being armed, the explosives around the plutonium core will not go off at the same time. My vision was not possible, but the explosion presented me with an opportunity that I have pursued relentlessly to this very day. An opportunity that you will help me realize."

"What do you mean?" Laia asked. She sounded angry, and that made me nervous. I didn't think it was a good idea to annoy this guy. "What makes you think we'll help you?"

At that moment, I thought we were going to die. Gorky stared at us, a cold look very much like what I imagine a mouse sees before a snake strikes. Then he laughed. "Plucky—I like that. Maria was the same. I could never persuade her to do anything she did not wish to do."

"Just as I will never help you," Laia said defiantly. I was immensely proud of her. I didn't have the courage to stand up to Gorky, mostly because I didn't think it would make any difference. I was beginning to suspect what Gorky wanted from us, and the stakes were so high that I doubted he would stop at anything to get what he wanted.

"Commendable," Gorky said with what appeared to be genuine admiration, "but I have a question for Steve." He looked at me with his cold gaze. "How much pain can you stand?"

I couldn't think of an answer, and it was all I could do not to collapse and plead for mercy under that relentless stare.

"A difficult question," Gorky acknowledged, his tone suddenly conversational. "A quick blow to the face, a broken nose, cracked ribs—I imagine you could handle a beating that involved those types of injuries, but they are crude. The secret to true pain is anticipation. A sudden blow hurts, but it is soon over. There may be fear of the next blow, but that takes time to build up, and we do not have too much time.

"Anticipation increases pain tenfold. For example, do you think you could stand having a fingernail pulled off slowly with a pair of pliers? Or having a finger slowly bent until the joint dislocates and the bone breaks? Even if you can stand these things once, you know that there are nine more digits awaiting attention."

Gorky turned to Laia. "Could you listen to Steve's screams as one of my friends destroyed his hands?"

Laia said nothing.

"What do you want?" I asked.

"Indeed, I should finish my story. I would hate you to suffer for nothing. Arturo's act over Palomares was dramatic, but it did not have the effect I had wished for. Instead of reacting with violent horror, the world sat enthralled for three months as the Americans searched for and then worked at recovering the lost fourth bomb. They almost became the heroes of the drama.

"Even worse, from my point of view, the Americans soon discovered Arturo's role in the incident. It was never made public, of course, but behind the scenes, immense efforts were made to discover who had employed him. I went on the run, changing my identity many times in the subsequent years and never staying in one place very long. I managed to stay one step ahead of the Americans, but my network was dismantled. Even Bob abandoned me, but through all those years of running and loneliness, there was something that kept me going.

"After I had delivered the explosives to Arturo, I did not return to France immediately. It was a dangerous thing to do, but I missed my homeland. I took the opportunity to check up on some of my sleepers. When the B-52 exploded, I knew Arturo was responsible and that it would not be long before he was discovered. I headed for the border but could not resist a brief stop in Barcelona to see Maria. She knew nothing of Arturo's role in the explosion or that he was one of my sleepers. I took great precautions to see that each sleeper knew as few others as possible.

"Maria was horrified at the incident and angry at the Americans for putting so many lives in danger. I was about to tell her of my role—to boast, I suppose—when Maria asked me if I remembered David McLean, the young Canadian soldier with the broken ribs. I said of course, and she told me that he had visited her only the day before. I was shocked, since I knew it was as big a risk for him to come back to Spain as it was for me. I asked Maria what David was doing here and she said he had been sent to try to find a saboteur and prevent a terrorist act. He had known the area targeted, and that planes were involved, but he'd had no idea what was going to happen until the B-52 exploded over Palomares. He had been depressed at his failure to stop the explosions, but he told Maria that he had hidden a fifth bomb.

"I encouraged Maria to talk, presenting myself as someone like her, who cared deeply for my fellow man. McLean and Maria had talked long about what he should do about the bomb. She argued that since the bomb was hidden in a place where no one would ever find it and was no threat to anyone, he should keep quiet about it. That way, it would be one less bomb that could be used to kill people. She said that he agreed not to tell anyone of the bomb's existence.

"I was thrilled when Maria told me this. I saw, in that hidden bomb, an opportunity to make the dramatic gesture that Arturo and I had dreamed of. Imagine a nuclear device detonated beneath the United Nations in New York or outside the Kremlin in Moscow or even here in Madrid! With that bomb, I could change the world. What time I had, I spent searching the world for David McLean and the hills above Palomares for the bomb. I found neither—until now. You will lead me to the bomb."

"What makes you think we know anything about it?" I asked. Gorky's story made sense and linked my grandfather to Palomares, but how could this old man possibly know who I was, let alone why Laia and I were here?

"I am old and not up to scrambling around the hills as I once could, but I have not totally given up hope. I have a modest apartment in Almería, and two days ago, I received an anonymous phone call identifying you two and telling me that you had the key to the bomb's location. The rest was easy—Palomares is not a large town. Lucio has been following you since you arrived."

"The guy on the red scooter?" Laia asked.

"Indeed. In fact, he would have followed you this morning straight to the location of the bomb—that is where you went, I assume—but he had mechanical troubles with his scooter. When he caught up with you, he phoned me, and we had to resort to this unpleasantness. But it is almost over. I have told you my story and, I hope, convinced you that I will stop at nothing to get what I want. Shall we go, or do I have to ask Lucio to begin removing fingernails?"

I shuddered at the mention of fingernails, but before I could think of anything to say, Laia spoke. "I will show you where the bomb is," she said calmly.

"You can't," I blurted out. "This maniac will set it off in the middle of a city somewhere. He could kill thousands of people."

"He might," Laia said, looking at me, "but what is certain is that I cannot sit and watch them torture you. I would tell them sooner or later, so why subject you to all that pain?" She seemed almost frighteningly calm, and what she said made logical sense. It was quite likely that I would tell Gorky where a hundred bombs were hidden after the first couple of fingernails had been ripped off. Even the simple threat of doing that to Laia would get me talking. It was wrong, but we weren't trained spies or secret agents. We were just a couple of scared kids. How could we be expected to stand up to torture by someone who had probably been trained by the KGB?

"Excellent decision," Gorky said, levering himself to his feet. "Let us go and get the fifth bomb."

EIGHTEEN

The drive back was more comfortable than the drive to the ruined building. We traveled more slowly, matching the pace of Gorky's rather old and battered Toyota—obviously, spying didn't pay very well. This time, Laia and I weren't blindfolded, and our feet weren't tied, but it was still difficult to stay balanced with our hands tied behind our backs. I had a moment of hope when I rolled heavily onto my cell phone and felt it vibrate, but there was no way I could reach it with my hands tied.

"Stop here," Laia ordered when we reached the point where the road was closest to location number five.

I let Laia lead the way as we worked our way around the hillside, wondering if she had some sort of escape plan in mind. I couldn't imagine what it might be. Our hands were still tied, and we were surrounded by four fit-looking men.

Progress was slow, with Gorky being helped along and having to take frequent breaks to catch his breath, but we eventually arrived at the rockfall. One of the Spaniards said something too fast for me to catch, and the others laughed. "What did he say?" I asked Laia.

"He said his grandfather used to say there were ghosts living here and that they used to steal sheep."

One of the other Spaniards looked over at me and said, "*Habrá fantasmas más pronto.*" I understood that. He had said there would be more ghosts soon. I really hoped Laia had a plan.

"Where is it?" Gorky asked. He was visibly excited now, looking around and waving his cane.

Laia led us over to rock fourteen. "You have to move that rock," she said.

Gorky gave orders, and two of his men hauled the rock aside. Gorky moved forward and peered into the dark hole. "Where is it?" he asked again, withdrawing his head. "I need a flashlight."

The Spaniards looked at each other and shrugged. Laia flashed me a warning look and shook her head very slightly. I realized that I was still wearing my backpack, held in place by my arms tied behind me. Our flashlight was still in it. I kept silent.

"It's in there," Laia said. "About three or four meters in. Untie my hands and I'll go get it."

Gorky looked uncertain, but he had little choice. Laia and I were the only two who could squeeze through the tiny hole, and enlarging it would be a big job. "Okay," he said. "I don't think you will escape into the hillside."

Lucio cut Laia's hands free. For a moment, she stood and massaged her wrists. She leaned toward me to give me a kiss on the cheek and whispered, "Come in fast as soon as they cut you free."

"Be careful," I said out loud, as I nodded to show that I understood what she had said.

"Very touching," Gorky said. "Now get me the bomb."

Laia squirmed through the hole and disappeared. I slowly edged forward, wriggling my hands to try and get the feeling back in them.

"I've found it," Laia shouted, her voice echoing out of the blackness. I thought Gorky was going to start dancing, he looked so strung out. All the men except Lucio had edged farther away from the hole, looking nervous. I guessed they weren't particularly keen on transporting a thermonuclear bomb in their van.

Laia grunted loudly. "What's wrong?" Gorky shouted.

"It's really heavy," Laia shouted back. "I can't move it on my own."

Gorky looked at his men. They knew what was coming and took a few shuffling steps back, shaking their heads. Gorky looked at Lucio. It was obvious that he would never get through the hole. "Do you have any rope in the van?" Gorky asked. Again the shuffling and head shaking. "You will go in and help your girlfriend," the old man said, turning back to me. "Cut him free," he ordered Lucio.

I stepped forward as Lucio drew a thin, evil-looking blade from his belt. As he sawed at my bonds, Gorky produced a small automatic pistol from his pocket. "Don't try anything funny," he warned.

"If you shoot me, you'll never get the bomb," I said, hoping I sounded confident enough to make the old man hesitate. My hands were free. I swung the backpack off my shoulders, held it in front of me and dived for the hole. The backpack was through and my shoulders were scraping painfully against the rocks when I heard Gorky shout something. I felt hands grabbing at my legs. I wriggled frantically, kicking my feet. My right foot connected with something solid, and I heard a satisfying cry of pain. The grip loosened, and I was through.

"This way," Laia urged from the blackness in front of me. "Against the wall on your right." I struggled to my knees, shoved the backpack in front of me and, ignoring my cuts and bruises, worked my way toward Laia's voice. There were some quite large rocks on the ground, and I kicked up a choking cloud of dust as I clambered over them. I tried not to think about what might be in the dust.

The light from the outside faded quickly, and I was in total darkness by the time I felt Laia's hand on mine. We fell into each other's arms, almost weeping with relief. "It'll take them a while to dig a hole big enough to get through," Laia said. "If we move a bit farther in, they'll never find us."

"This was a brilliant idea," I said. "Was the bomb actually heavy?"

"I don't know," Laia replied. "It's a nuclear bomb! I stayed as far away as possible, hard up against the opposite wall from where we spotted it earlier. I never even saw it."

I began to laugh, as much from the release of tension as anything. I was almost hysterical, but Gorky's voice sobered me up quickly. "Come out. Bring the bomb with you and no harm will befall you."

Laia and I huddled silently against the wall. "I will give you one final warning," Gorky shouted. I could see a shadow partly blocking the patch of daylight. It seemed far away.

The crack of a pistol shot was deafening in the confined space of the tunnel. "Come out now," Gorky ordered. His voice was followed by two more shots. I thought I heard a bullet whine past, and I tried to push us both into the wall at our backs.

"Move deeper in," I said in an urgent whisper. As quietly as possible, we worked our way farther into the darkness, until we turned a corner and couldn't see the hole anymore. There were no more shots. We sat with our backs against the rough stone of the wall. "I think we're safe here," Laia said. "Let's get the flashlight and see where we are."

I fumbled with the zipper of the backpack. "A drink of water would be nice too," I said as I felt around for the rubber tube of the flashlight. The beam looked incredibly bright after the pitch darkness. I shone the light into the bag and brought out our water and two granola bars. We ate and drank thankfully.

"I don't suppose your cell phone has a signal in here," Laia said through a mouthful of granola bar.

"I doubt it," I said, but I pulled the phone from my jeans pocket. There was no signal, but the phone was on and there was a text from DJ. what's up? You called but no one there. DJ.

"I must have pocket-dialed him when I was rolling around in the van. I wish I'd known—DJ could have come and rescued us."

Laia laughed. "Felip might have been a more useful call."

"I would even have settled for Chad," I said. "He would have distracted Gorky by trying to sell him something."

We both laughed, enjoying the brief release of tension, and then Laia became serious again. "Do you think they were really going to kill us?"

"I think they were," I said, equally serious. "The bomb means a lot to Gorky. He wants to do something terrible with it because he has this crazy idea that it will change the world. I can see why Grandfather insisted on keeping the bomb hidden from him. Gorky won't want to leave any witnesses."

"Do you think he's really mad?' Laia asked.

"Yes," I replied without a moment's hesitation. "He's totally insane. The bomb's become a complete obsession with him. I don't know if he could even set the thing off. Felip told us it was very difficult to trigger a nuclear explosion." But then I thought of something else Felip had told us. "He doesn't need to set it off. Didn't Felip say that plutonium *dust* is what is really deadly? Something about only a thousandth of a gram being enough to kill you? If Gorky can get the plutonium out of the bomb, he could grind it up and pass it through the heating system of a building, or put it in a water supply, or even just throw handfuls into the air in the middle of a crowded city. He could kill thousands of people without any kind of explosion."

NINETEEN

We sat in silence for a moment, contemplating the horrors of what Gorky could do. "I don't see how we can stop him," Laia said at last.

"Neither do I. All we can do is wait here and hope he leaves. Then we can go and tell the police about it. With any luck, they'll catch him before he does any damage."

"Where exactly is *here*?" Laia asked. I shone the torch around.

We were in a low-roofed, narrow tunnel. If I stretched my arms out, I could almost touch both walls at once, and there wasn't enough height to stand upright.

The roof and walls were fairly smooth, but here and there, chunks of rock had fallen to the floor. Behind us, the tunnel sloped gradually up and curved away to the hole we had entered. Ahead, the tunnel was more level and headed off into the hill.

Laia answered her own question. "It's a mine."

"How old do you think it is?"

"Who knows? Maybe a few hundred years, or even Roman or Carthaginian."

"Do you think there's another way out?" I asked.

"I doubt it," Laia said. "In any case, it's probably not a good idea to go wandering around."

I was about to agree when I heard a noise. "What was that?"

"I think Gorky's trying to enlarge the hole," Laia said.

"I'll have a look," I said, switching the flashlight off. Slowly, I crawled back to where the tunnel curved. I peered up the slope. Someone was working on the rocks around the edge of the hole. The noise we had heard was from rocks falling into the tunnel. I could see the shadow of a figure moving back and forth in front of the hole, which already looked bigger.

I was about to turn around when I heard the faint sound of shouting outside, followed by more pistol shots. I crawled back to Laia as fast as I could. "Something's going on outside," I said. "There's a lot of shouting and gunshots."

"No one seemed too keen on coming in here," Laia said thoughtfully. "Maybe Gorky's trying to encourage them."

"Maybe. In any case, I think we should move farther in. If it stays a single tunnel, we can't get lost."

Moving through the tunnel was easier with the flashlight, but we didn't get far. One more corner, and we came to a serious cave-in. A large section of the roof had collapsed, completely blocking the tunnel. We had passed no side tunnels, so all we could do was sit and wait.

"They don't have a flashlight," I said, not sure whether I was trying to reassure Laia or myself. "They won't come this far in."

"Of course not," Laia agreed, but she didn't sound convinced. "It wouldn't make sense."

It didn't make sense, but then, we had agreed that Gorky was crazy. Not much of anything he did made sense. We turned the flashlight off to save the battery and sat in the darkness. It was impossible to tell how long we had sat before I heard another noise. At first I thought it was rats, but it soon became obvious that it was something larger. "Someone's coming," I hissed.

"I can hear them," Laia replied. We could see a dull glow coming from around the corner, gradually getting brighter. "He's got a flashlight," Laia said. Now we were in an even worse spot than being tied up in the ruined room. We were deep in a blocked tunnel with nowhere to go and no way to defend ourselves, being stalked by an insane guy with a gun.

"Do you think it's Gorky?" I asked.

"He couldn't make it all the way down here. It's probably Lucio or one of the others."

Great, I thought. There goes our chance of wrestling the gun away from him.

"Pick up some stones," I said. "As soon as he comes around the corner, start throwing. Aim for his head."

I felt around on the ground and picked up three pieces of rock, each about the size of an egg. Laia moved over to give us each room to throw. I got as ready as I could. The light was quite bright now. Where had Gorky found a powerful flashlight?

The light came around the corner and swung toward us. "Now!" I shouted. I aimed for just above the light, where I guessed the man's head must be. We both threw as hard as we could. I heard one stone clatter off the tunnel wall, but that wasn't what stopped me from throwing a second stone. It was the voice coming out of the darkness behind the light. "Ow! Hey! Cut it out, you kids!" a familiar voice shouted. "I'm here to help you."

"Chad?" Laia and I said at the same instant.

"Of course it's Chad," the voice said. "Who did you think would come crawling all this way in to find you?" The flashlight swung up and illuminated the smiling face. There was a thin trickle of blood running down his forehead. If there had been enough room to run forward and hug Chad, I would have. Right then, I would have put everything I had into one of his investment schemes. "Have you finished throwing things?"

"Yes," I said. "It's good to see you. You're bleeding. Sorry I hit you."

"It's nothing. You've got a good arm, kid. With room for a decent windup, I wouldn't be talking to you right now. Are you kids okay?"

"We are," Laia said. "What are you doing here?"

"I'm the cavalry come to rescue you," Chad said, a laugh in his voice. "But let's get back outside. My claustrophobia doesn't like narrow tunnels under mountains."

I switched on our flashlight, and we worked our way back. The hole had been considerably enlarged, so much so that we didn't need our flashlights for the last few meters. "Where's the bomb?" Laia asked.

"All things will be explained in time," Chad said cheerily.

A ragged round of applause greeted us as we emerged onto the hillside. I blinked in the bright daylight and looked around. The first things I noticed were Gorky's thugs, sitting in a miserable group, guarded by a Spanish policeman. Nearby, also guarded by a policeman, Lucio sat on a rock, having a wound in his shoulder treated by a paramedic. Beside him was a body on a stretcher, covered in a white sheet. Uniformed police and men in civilian clothes were spread around, and several ATVs were parked behind them. A helicopter thumped in circles overhead.

"What's going on?" I asked.

Before Chad could answer, a figure pushed through the crowd and ran to embrace Laia. "Are you okay?" Felip asked.

"I'm fine," Laia said.

Felip looked over at me. "Me too," I said. A paramedic came over and began examining our cuts and bruises. She swabbed the cuts clean and put ointment and bandages on the worst ones. I was so stunned that I was happy simply to sit and be attended to while my brain tried to work its way around what had happened.

"Who's under the sheet?" Laia asked. It was something I had been wondering too.

"It's the old guy with one arm," Felip said.

"Did they shoot him?"

"No," Felip answered, "although he did fire a couple of rounds at the police when they arrived. The police fired back, and that's how the big guy got shot." He nodded toward the sullen Lucio. "The old guy just folded. He was dead before anyone got to him. I think it was his heart."

So that explained the shooting I had heard from inside the tunnel. It was the police arriving. I laughed.

"What?" Laia asked.

"We were hiding from the police when we went farther along the tunnel."

Laia smiled. "I was hiding from Chad," she said.

"Who *is* he?" I asked.

"And *where* is he?" Laia added.

As if on cue, Chad appeared from one of the ATVs. He had wiped the blood off his forehead and was carrying the bomb in front of him. Both Laia and I jumped to our feet. "What are you doing?" I shouted.

Chad smiled—and dropped the bomb. As it hit the ground, he swung his right foot and volleyed it straight at me. Instinctively, I put my hands out and caught it—and found myself holding a battered leather soccer ball.

"This isn't the bomb," I said. "What happened to the bomb?"

"There was no bomb," Chad said with a smile. "Just an old soccer ball that someone lost once."

"That makes no sense," I said. I looked around for confirmation. Laia was frowning at Chad. Felip gently shook his head.

I looked back at Chad. "There is no bomb," he repeated, his smile gone and his voice hard. "You kids have had an exciting and scary day, running into the middle of this drug deal. You were lucky you could get into the tunnel before the shooting started. I have a couple of details to tidy up, and the press will be here soon. Felip will take you back to the hotel for a shower and a rest. We'll meet for dinner later—say, nine o'clock," he added, looking at Felip. "I'll explain what's going on then. Okay?" The way he said "okay" didn't allow for anything other than acceptance.

I looked at Laia. "Okay," she said.

"Okay," I agreed.

"Excellent." Chad stepped forward and shook my hand. It was an awkward gesture, but I felt a crumpled piece of paper in his palm. He winked at me. I took the paper and slipped it into my pocket as Chad led us over to Felip's car. Several of the police patted us on the shoulder as we passed. I ignored them, my mind struggling desperately to understand. It couldn't all have been some horrible misunderstanding—could it? And what was in the note from Chad?

TWENTY

On the way back to the hotel, Laia and I bombarded Felip with questions, but we didn't learn much. Felip had been on his way back from Almería when Chad had called him and told him to meet us all here in the hills. Felip had arrived on the hillside after it was all over and the hole had been widened enough to allow Chad in. He didn't know much more than we did, but he was so happy that we were okay that he didn't seem interested in questioning anything. Even after I'd given him the outline of the story that Gorky told us and Laia had wondered out loud why Chad seemed to be so tight with the Spanish police, all he said was, "I'm sure Chad will clear up all the details over dinner."

It was late afternoon when we made it back to the hotel, although it felt as if it had been weeks since Laia and I left that morning. I was so confused and tired that I hardly noticed the naked people criss-crossing the lobby as I headed for the elevator. Felip saw us to the elevator and suggested we have a nap and a shower before meeting for dinner.

As soon as the elevator doors closed, I took the crumpled paper out of my pocket. "What's that?" Laia asked.

"Chad gave it to me," I replied, smoothing it out. The note said, *You and Laia meet me in the bar at eight o'clock. Don't tell Felip.*

"I guess he wants to tell us something he doesn't want Felip to hear," Laia said.

"Yeah," I agreed, "and I'm fine with that. I just want to know what's going on."

Laia and I went to our rooms. I sat on my bed, determined to think things through and try to make sense of it all. I failed. I set my alarm and immediately fell into a deep sleep. When I woke up it was dark, and every square inch of my body ached. It was seven forty-five. I dragged myself into the shower.

The hot water stung my cuts, but I didn't care. My nap had refreshed me, but I still felt like my world had been turned upside down. Ever since DJ had sent the pages from Grandfather's notebook, trying to understand what they meant had been our focus. We had been threatened and kidnapped, but we had done well. We had broken the code, worked out what the locations were and what their significance was, fitted all the bits (including the story Gorky had told us) into a coherent narrative that explained most, if not all, of what we had been given. There had been nothing about a drug deal. Now this mystery man, Chad, who kept showing up in the most unexpected places, was saying that everything we thought we understood was meaningless. I refused to believe that we'd been wrong every step of the way—but it *had* been a soccer ball Chad kicked to me, that I was sure of.

Another idea crossed my mind. Had Grandfather organized this as a joke? If he had, it was incredibly elaborate and expensive. Was it some kind of test? A joke or a test. Neither seemed likely, given the lengths Grandfather would have had to go to. And how could he possibly have known that his grandsons would be the ones to find the stuff in the cabin? I was so confused that any wild idea was up for grabs.

As I gently dabbed my painful cuts dry and wandered back out to my bedroom, I had an idea. Picking up the TV remote, I flipped through the channels until I found the news. The first thing I saw was a shot of the hillside, taken from a helicopter; there were figures and vehicles all around. You could see hooded men, one with his arm in a sling, being bundled into police cars; a stretcher with a body on it was being loaded into an ambulance. I had to concentrate to try to understand what the commentator was saying. There was nothing about a bomb. I grasped enough to understand that there had been a drug bust in the hills. The police chief said something about a tipoff, and then a politician talked about how Spain must clamp down on the growing problem of drugs being smuggled in through the local ports. Then the news moved on to the upcoming Real Madrid versus Barcelona soccer game. What was going on? The bomb—or the soccer ball—was being hushed up, written out of the story. I turned the TV off, and as I dressed, I promised myself that I wouldn't stop questioning Chad until I got the whole story out of him.

As it turned out, I hardly had to ask a single question.

Just before eight I knocked on Laia's door, and we headed down to the bar together. On the way, I only had time to tell her what I had heard and seen on the TV and confirm that she was as confused by it as I was. Chad was waiting for us in a booth. He stood up as we approached. I opened my mouth to say something, but he got the first word in. "Before you say anything," he said, "I want to apologize. I have lied to you both and used you shamelessly. I cannot expect forgiveness, but I ask that you listen to what I have to say. I hope you will at least then understand."

I looked at Laia; we both nodded.

"Excellent," Chad said as we sat. "First, what would you like to drink?"

"Kas," Laia and I said.

"Okay," Chad said. "While I get them, you should probably read this. It was taped underneath the soccer ball." He handed me an envelope. There was nothing written on it. Laia and I moved closer together, and I carefully lifted the flap and pulled out two sheets of paper. Both pages were covered with tight, neat writing that sent a shiver through me even before I read the first word. This was a letter from Grandfather.

I have no idea who will read this, if anyone, but if you are standing in the Spanish sunshine, wondering why you have just found a soccer ball inside a Roman mine, you deserve some kind of an explanation.

It is unlikely that you have stumbled across this; therefore, you have followed a trail of clues to reach this point. I intend to leave clues to this and to other aspects of my complex and secret life in a secure place. If that is how you have found this, then I will be long dead, and I offer you my posthumous congratulations. If your code name is that of a Russian writer, then I say—too late.

There was a time in 1938 when I was convinced I could never return to Spain, but now, in 1975, with Franco on his deathbed, I find I am back for the third time. I passed briefly through during the Second World War, I was here in 1966, and now I am back. Of course, I have never been back as myself. During the war I had no identity; I was a shadow passing through the landscape by night. The other two visits have been as Pedro Martinez.

For those of us who survived Spain in the 1930s, it was hard to give up the fight. Some, like Kim Philby—whom I met in 1938 outside Barcelona when he was, supposedly, a reporter and I was about to be repatriated—had already chosen sides and simply continued the secret work they were doing. Others, like my fellow survivor Bob and myself, were less certain. The world after Hitler and Mussolini were defeated was a complex place. I missed the certainty of what we had fought for in Spain, and however hard I searched, I could find no cause that promised a better world. I was approached by the Soviets, but by then I knew a little of what Stalin had done to those who disagreed with him, so I turned them down.

Several months after that, Bob came to visit me. He told me that the Soviets had approached him as well and that he had accepted their offer. He asked if I would work beside him. Again I said no.

The very next day, I was visited by an American, a rather brash young man, who suggested that I keep in loose contact with Bob, but that I work for him. We talked a long time, and he was very persuasive, presenting the work I would do not as picking one side or the other, but rather as finding and using information to maintain a balance in the world. He said it was futile to try and make the world a better place, and that the best we could hope for was to stop it from getting any worse. I thought long and hard before I accepted his suggestion, and I drew the line at becoming a full double agent, but I guess I liked the idea of being in touch with both sides. Of course, it never worked out as simply as I had expected, and every job I did had its own issues and drew me deeper and deeper into this strange secret life I find myself in now.

In any case, shortly after Christmas of 1965, I was contacted by my young friend and told that I had to go back to Spain. He had word of a plot to sabotage a plane carrying nuclear weapons. Despite my identity as Pedro Martinez, I was very nervous, but I went. I met our information source in Spain and for the first time learned of Gorky and his network. I didn't agree with the American nuclear policy, but what Gorky was trying to do was madness. I came and based myself in Palomares in hopes that Gorky would show himself. I could think of nothing else to do.

Every day, I came into the hills to watch the B-52s refueling, and the rest of my time I spent traveling around, listening, trying to find the slightest hint of who Gorky was or where he might be. I talked with everyone I met, including the shepherds in the hills. I learned many fascinating stories, one of which led me to the ancient mine where you discovered the ball.

Unfortunately, my attempts to prevent the sabotage failed. The planes did blow up and the bombs fell—thank God they didn't explode. Some of the bombs did, however, break apart, and the plutonium core from one landed close by. Knowing Gorky was somewhere nearby and would do anything to obtain this weapon, I hid it in the mine.

I didn't know who I could trust. Remember, these were very paranoid times. We all thought we were on the brink of destroying the world. Children used to practice hiding under their desks for when the bombs dropped. There were books and films about an accident or a mistake triggering nuclear war. I didn't want the bomb I had found to fall into the wrong hands.

After I hid the bomb, I left Palomares quickly. The area was crawling with police and American soldiers, and the chances of my real identity being discovered were too great. However, I did take a risk. I went to Barcelona and visited Maria. I told her what I had done. That was probably a mistake, but seeing her again after all those years was wonderful. We talked all night. She said that I should leave the bomb hidden so that it could never be used by anyone. She said that it would be a tiny piece of good I could do to make the world a better place. I agreed. I think that night, seeing Maria again, I would have agreed to turn myself in to Franco's police if she had asked me.

I left Maria as the sun was rising, and it was the hardest thing I have ever done. But I had to get out of Spain, and I had a wife and family back in Canada. Why is it that life leaves so many loose ends? But I am wallowing in nostalgia and becoming maudlin. This will be of little interest to you, whoever you may be, so I must complete my tale.

After I crossed the Spanish border, reported to the young American and told him the whole story, omitting only that I had hidden the bomb, I returned to Canada and had as much of a normal life as I could manage in those strange days.

As the years passed, Gorky's name cropped up from time to time. I realized that when he was not on the run from the Americans, he was hunting me. There could be only one reason: the bomb. Somehow he had discovered its existence and thought I knew its location. Now it was too dangerous to leave it in the cave. I resurrected Pedro Martinez and came back to Spain. I will replace the bomb with the soccer ball and this note, place the bomb close to Morón Air Base and phone in an anonymous tip. The Americans will no doubt dispose of the bomb quietly. There are no more nuclear-armed B-52s in the sky—we have more efficient ways of killing each other now.

I don't know how much of this, if any, will make sense to you, but I need to set the story down. I will write other things down in other places in case the day ever comes when I have to justify any of the things I have done.

I will return home now and devote my time to my family. They, after all, are what is truly important. I will not visit Maria again.

David McLean

TWENTY-ONE

Laia and I sat and stared at the letter long after we had finished reading. I had choked up. Grandfather was telling me another piece of his life. I knew he had no idea when he wrote it that I would be the one to read it, but that didn't matter. It was still him talking to me.

"It's not fair," I said. "Why is it only after he dies that I get to know Grandfather and the extraordinary things he did?"

Laia reached over and squeezed my hand. "He *was* an amazing man," she said. "I wonder what the others are finding out about him."

I sniffed loudly and looked up from the letter. Chad had returned with our drinks and was sitting across from me, a faint smile on his lips. He looked different, older, more relaxed, like an actor who has finished a role and taken off a mask. "Who are you?" I asked.

Chad's smile broadened, emphasizing the wrinkles around his eyes. "I'm the brash young man your grandfather mentions in the letter." Even his voice was different—deeper, more mature.

"You're not old enough," I blurted out. When I'd met Chad in the plane, I had guessed he was in his fifties or sixties, which would have made him a teenager in 1966, and Grandfather had been recruited by the young man sometime before that.

"In my business, you never retire. There are too many loose ends that can come back to haunt you. So I keep myself in shape, and since I'm afraid my one weakness is vanity"—Chad pulled the skin around his eyes until the wrinkles disappeared—"I have had some chemical and surgical help. I'm not going to see seventy again."

"What *is* your business, exactly?" Laia asked. "You're not an investment counselor or an international real-estate advisor."

"You're correct, I am neither of those things, although I pride myself on the depth of knowledge I have picked up over the years in both those fields. Broadly, I am an employee of the American government. I would rather not go into details, as I am sure you understand, but if I can rely on your discretion, I can fill you in on some background pertaining to your grandfather."

Both Laia and I nodded.

"Excellent. I was what's called a child prodigy—I was reading Shakespeare at age four and performing calculus by age seven, that sort of thing. My parents were well-off, so I was pushed through a very expensive, very high-powered education program. I completed a university degree at fifteen and my doctorate at eighteen. I take no credit for this—my brain is merely a freak of nature. Learning just comes easily to me. What I really wanted was to become an actor like Marlon Brando or Humphrey Bogart, but my achievements had attracted attention. I was approached by the US government and persuaded to work for them. They made it sound important and interesting, and gave me the impression that it would only be for a few years. Of course, that last bit was a lie."

A look of regret flashed across Chad's face, and I wondered what he could have done if the government hadn't got its claws into him. I was certain he lived with that question every day.

"One of my first tasks was to meet with David McLean and see if he would work for us. I managed to persuade him—and in the process learned that acting was in fact a large part of what I would be required to do. No Oscar nominations though." Chad's smile returned fleetingly. "I enjoyed working with your grandfather very much. He was an intelligent man, and I have always admired that. David McLean required good, rational reasons for everything he did. Some of the people I hired simply required a paycheck at the end of each month. Bob was one of those."

"Bob!" I said. "The Bob who was with Grandfather in Spain and worked for Gorky?"

"The very same."

"He was a double agent?"

"And a very good one," Chad said. "Unfortunately, he was betrayed by someone—we think it may have been Kim Philby—and died in a mysterious car crash. Gorky's network was not as tight as he would like to think; a number of our agents infiltrated it."

"Was Maria one?" Laia interrupted.

Chad shook his head. "We approached her, of course, but she was a very strong woman with a clear moral code, and she refused. I think she used Gorky much more than he did her." Chad smiled, as if remembering a pleasant experience. "However, you may recognize another of our agents, Arturo."

"The saboteur at Morón Air Base?" I asked.

"There was no saboteur at Morón."

"But the planes exploded," Laia said.

"Gorky did have a plan," Chad explained, "but Arturo told us about it. I sent your grandfather down to see if he could find out who was supplying the explosives and see if it would lead us to Gorky. He was becoming too dangerous, so we decided to close him down."

I wondered what exactly *close him down* meant, but I said, "Except Grandfather failed. There was a bomb on the plane."

"He did not find Gorky, that's true, but there was no bomb on the plane. The explosion above Palomares was simply what everyone said it was: a terrible accident. We think the tanker got too close and the fuel line punctured the skin of the B-52 behind the cockpit, causing the explosion that took both planes down."

I stared at Chad. Was he telling the truth? There was no way to know. He had taken his interest in becoming an actor seriously. "What about the lost bomb?" I asked.

"We could never work out what had happened to the plutonium core from bomb number three. We calculated that it should have landed in the hills, but extensive searches never turned it up. Eventually, we assumed it must have become entangled in one of the parachutes and drifted out to sea. We gave up searching for it. We did not know that David had visited Maria on the way home from Palomares and that she had persuaded him to leave the bomb a secret. Nor did we know that Gorky had visited Maria the next day and that she had let slip the bomb's existence. We thought Gorky and his network were neutralized, but in reality, he was searching for the bomb and becoming more fanatical and obsessed every year.

"I became involved in other things, most of which had nothing to do with David McLean. The events of that January in Spain faded. As I said, one never retires in this business, but you do ease off with age. Earlier this year, I was on a beach in Florida when I received a phone call from your grandfather. We chatted about old times and he told me about you seven boys and the plans he had for you." Chad was smiling broadly as he talked about Grandfather. "It was so typical of him to give you all mysterious envelopes. Anyway, he ended the conversation by telling me about hiding the bomb in the hills. I was horrified and asked him where it was. He laughed and said that I probably had a better idea than he did. Then he hung up.

"I was confused and traveled up to Canada to ask him what he meant. I didn't think there was a tearing rush. But there was. I arrived the day after David McLean died. With him died the location of the bomb.

"Of course, I realize now what happened. Your grandfather assumed I knew that the bomb had been returned to Morón Air Base, hence his comment about me knowing where it was. Trouble was, the Air Force never told anyone about retrieving the bomb; they simply disposed of it in our storage facility in the Utah desert. I guess they didn't want an embarrassing incident from the past brought up and had no idea it might be important. So, there I was, convinced there was still a nuclear bomb hidden in the hills above Palomares. That's where you come in."

"How?" I asked.

"After David died, I set up surveillance on you and your cousins."

"You what?" I almost shouted. "I was being watched all this time? That's illegal!"

Chad laughed. "I'm sorry," he said when he had finished, "but after what I've told you, do you think legality is a large part of the work I do? In any case"—he held up a hand before I could launch in again—"no one was watching you; we simply followed your movements by putting tags on your passport number and bank-card use. It's quite easy.

"We did take more notice when we saw that your envelope was bringing you to Spain and"—Chad looked at Laia—"when we saw you were meeting Maria's great-granddaughter, we did crank up the interest level a bit. Interest faded when we discovered you weren't coming anywhere near Palomares— by the way, I would love to read your grandfather's journal one day—but you remained on our radar.

When we saw you were coming back to Spain, I booked the seat beside you on the last leg of your flight and arranged the meeting with Felip to see if we could get you here and find out anything.

"We knew Gorky was still alive and living in Almería. He was harmless as long as the bomb remained hidden, so we let him be. Yesterday, after you two went off to look for where the bombs landed, Felip told me a bit about the mysterious codes you were following. I guessed immediately what they must be, and I had a problem: Palomares is a small town, and Gorky might find out what was going on. I decided to pre-empt him."

Chad stopped talking and looked down at the table. He looked almost guilty, not a feeling I associated with him. "What happened then?" I encouraged him.

Chad looked up. "I phoned Gorky and told him what was going on."

It took me a moment to work out what that meant. "You told him we were here and knew where the bomb was?" I almost yelled, realizing that Chad's phone call was how the guy on the red scooter had found us and how Gorky had managed to kidnap us. "You could have got us killed!"

"It was supposed to be under control," Chad said miserably. Was his guilt an act as well? I was furious.

"Well, it wasn't under control, was it?" I said, banging my fist on the table. The barman glanced over at us.

Chad shrugged. "I did try to take precautions. When I bumped into you last night, I'd just finished adding sugar to the red scooter's gas tank. I figured that would slow them down a bit."

"So that's how Lucio lost us," I said. "He couldn't follow us up the hill until he had fixed his scooter."

"We were going to track you using your GPS signal," Chad went on. "When Gorky contacted you, we could move in. That way we would have the bomb and Gorky."

"But we didn't take the GPS with us this morning," Laia said. "Felip had it."

"Exactly," Chad agreed. "We lost you in the hills—until you made a cell-phone call."

"I didn't...oh, the pocket-dial to DJ," I said. "You were monitoring my cell phone. When I rolled over in the van and speed-dialed DJ by mistake, you could zero in on the signal."

Chad nodded. "We lost the signal soon after, but by then the chopper was in the air and we had a fairly close location for you. You must have just gone into the mine when we came over the hill—the cavalry to the rescue," he added weakly. "Only Lucio and Gorky tried to put up any kind of fight, and that didn't last long. I'm sorry Gorky had a heart attack," Chad said as if talking about an old friend. "I should very much like to have had a conversation with him."

"Well, we talked to him," I said, still angry that we had been used as bait to draw out Gorky. "It wasn't that much fun."

"I'm really sorry," Chad said. "If there's anything I can do to make it up to you…"

I was thinking free tickets to the Barcelona versus Real Madrid soccer game, but Laia was more practical. "There's a Russian guy," she said, "probably Mafia. He owns most of the hotels and resorts around here. He has very pale blue eyes."

"Vladislav Gorev. We know about him."

"Then why don't you stop him?" I asked, still angry. "He's corrupt, he hires thugs to do his dirty work, and he's probably into drug dealing."

"All of those things are true," Chad admitted, "but it's an internal Spanish matter. We can't interfere."

"Anyway," Laia said, "this guy and a couple of his thugs threatened us. They gave us forty-eight hours to talk Felip into convincing you that buying land here isn't a good idea. He doesn't want competition."

"And you would like that problem to go away?" Chad asked. "There are no Americans who want to buy the land. That was just a cover for me to contact Felip. I will have a word with Vlad. No problem."

"Vlad! Are you friends?" I asked.

Chad smiled. "We've done business together. Anyway, I am real sorry for the trouble I got you guys into," Chad said, reverting to his sleazy real-estate persona. "I'm sure glad that it all worked out okay. It's been a real pleasure meeting both you folks, and if you ever have a yearning for some real estate or investment advice, who you gonna call?"

TWENTY-TWO

Dinner that evening was amazing. Chad paid for everything and insisted that we eat the best, most expensive things on the menu. I was certainly going to have trouble adjusting to chili, mac and cheese, and the occasional burger when I got home. Afterward, Laia and I went for what was becoming our habitual evening stroll along the beach.

"If Chad had become an actor," I commented, "he'd have a mantel loaded with Oscars by now. Do you think we can believe anything he says?"

"I think he more or less told us the truth in the bar," Laia said. "He had nothing to gain by lying."

"Yeah, but he told Felip a different story over dinner."

"It wasn't that different," Laia said. "Chad just left a lot of stuff out. I'm sure Felip didn't believe everything he said, but I doubt he'll complain, especially after Chad offered to use his connections to help get the Americans to pay for a proper cleanup in Palomares."

"I suppose so," I agreed. I was still annoyed that Chad had used us to trap Gorky, but he'd also rescued us and he'd helped me fill in a lot of background on Grandfather's mysterious past. "I wonder what the others are finding out about Grandfather's secret life," I said.

"He certainly was an interesting man," Laia said. "And at least we proved he wasn't a traitor."

"According to Chad," I pointed out. "He's probably not the most reliable witness, and, as we found out, in the world Grandfather lived in, the line between treachery and loyalty is very blurred—a treacherous act by one person is a loyal act by another. In all of this, only Maria seems to have had a moral code that she stuck to despite everything."

"She was a very strong woman," Laia agreed. "I'm glad we discovered a little about her past as well as your grandfather's."

"Me too." I glanced at Laia walking beside me. The lights from the hotels and waterfront bars illuminated her smile as she turned to look at me. "Do you think that every time we meet, we are destined to find out something else about our families' pasts?" she asked.

"I hope so," I replied, thrilled by the idea that we would meet many more times. "Mind you, I hope there's a little less excitement and violence next time. I could do without that. I still shudder when I think of Lucio with a pair of pliers in his hand, hovering over my fingernails."

Laia laughed and squeezed my hand. "Or Scarface pointing a gun at your head."

I nodded. "At least Chad will get us out of that mess with Blue Eyes."

"Let's hope so."

We stopped walking and stood, staring out to sea. The lights of scattered ships bobbed on the horizon, and a low, full moon painted a broad, shimmering silver path across the water. "You know, despite everything," I said, "these past few days have been among the best of my life."

"Mine too. But there's a problem for you." Laia had suddenly turned serious.

"What?" I asked, worried.

"It really puts pressure on you to organize something special for next summer when I come and visit you in Canada."

"Oh, we can do excitement and violence in Canada," I said with a laugh. "Bunny has some interesting gang contacts—and have you ever been to a hockey game?"

The next morning, Laia and I were sitting in the lobby of the Puesta del Sol, surrounded by our bags, waiting for Felip to come down. We had said goodbye to Chad over breakfast and were looking forward to a normal tourist day, seeing the sights of Cartagena.

"I hardly notice the naked people anymore," I said as a bare, chattering family strolled past us.

"So are you ready for a swim now?' Laia asked with a mischievous smile.

"Not quite yet," I said.

I was staring idly at the elevator doors when they slid open and Tattoo Head stepped out and came toward us. It never even crossed my mind that Chad might not have managed to contact Blue Eyes and that an unpleasant revenge might be heading our way. Tattoo Head was naked, and his head was not the only part of his body tattooed. In fact, there was barely a square centimeter of un-inked skin to be seen amid the riot of reds, blues, greens, yellows and blacks that covered his body. The man was a walking art gallery, and the tattoo artist had had a large canvas to work with.

Green vines wound around Tattoo Head's legs, strange mythical creatures peering out through the foliage. Blue and yellow serpents coiled up his arms, fangs bared and red eyes burning. On his chest, a dark, cowled skull grimaced against a background of spiraling galaxies and exploding stars. Everything seemed alive as the man's muscles moved when he walked.

Laia gasped, and my mouth hung open in awe. I hardly noticed that Tattoo Head was walking right up to us. About a meter away, he stopped and spun slowly around. His back was as impressive as his front: a blue-and-purple cobra wound its way around the horned face of a demon that stretched from his neck to his waist.

"You like tattoos?" Tattoo Head asked when he turned to face us. He was grinning like a child showing off his newest toy.

All I could do was nod dumbly. Laia managed to say, "It's incredible."

Tattoo Head beamed with pleasure. "I have present," he said in a heavy Russian accent. "From Vladislav." He reached into the bag that hung from one shoulder. I thought for a second that he was going to pull out a gun, but he handed me a small package. "Have good day," Tattoo Head said as he turned and headed for the door to the pool.

"That was amazing," I managed to say after the cobra and demon had disappeared to impress the unsuspecting guests poolside.

"Now, that would be a torture," Laia observed, "having your entire body tattooed like that."

"At least you'd have something to show for it in the end," I said.

"What did he give you?" Laia asked.

I unwrapped the package to find a book—*The Collected Short Stories of Maxim Gorky*. I laughed out loud and showed it to Laia. "Lorca and Gorky," she said. "It's been a literary few days as well."

I opened the book. On the title page, Blue Eyes had written:

For the stories you haven't yet read.

Enjoy.

Vladislav Gorev

I smiled and flipped through a few pages. A folded sheet of paper fell out. Laia picked it up and unfolded it. It was a letter, handwritten and obviously old. The text was in Russian script, but the signature and date at the bottom were understandable. The signature was Maxim Gorky's, and the date was 1917.

"That's the real gift," Laia said. "It's probably worth a lot. I think maybe it's Blue Eyes's way of apologizing."

"I wonder if it's in code," I said.

ACKNOWLEDGMENTS

Once more, thanks to Eric for his drive and dedication; Andrew for letting us keep the story going; and Sarah for again making sure seven diverse, creative people are on the same page.

JOHN WILSON grew up on the Isle of Skye and outside Glasgow in Scotland without the slightest idea that he would ever write books. After a degree in geology from St. Andrews University, he worked in Zimbabwe and Alberta before taking up writing full-time and moving out to Lantzville on Vancouver Island in 1991. John is addicted to history and firmly believes that the past must have been just as exciting, confusing and complex to those who lived through it as our world is to us. John has written over forty books of fiction and nonfiction for kids, teens and adults, and he has won or been shortlisted for many awards, including the Governor General's, Geoffrey Bilson, Red Maple and White Pine. John spends significant portions of his year traveling across the country, telling stories and getting young readers (particularly but not exclusively boys) excited about the past. *Broken Arrow* is the sequel to *Lost Cause*, John's novel in Seven (the series). For more information, please visit johnwilsonauthor.com.

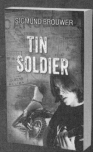